RYAN SEACREST IS FAMOUS

RYAN SEACREST IS FAMOUS

stories by dave housley

IM·PE·TUS press

Impetus Press
PO Box 10025
Iowa City, IA 52240
www.impetuspress.com
info@impetuspress.com

978-0-9776693-4-9

cover design and
text layout by Willy Blackmore

October 2007

Table of Contents

Bare

I shaved my balls a day after Claire left. A few weeks later, the bottom of the shaft. By the time her mail stopped coming and the telemarketers had finally deleted my number from their database, I was bare as a coffee cup.

We had grown apart since sometime around when the dog died. I took it hard. I quit my job, cashed out my 401K, started listening to Pink Floyd again, asked myself big dark questions I couldn't answer. I was thirty.

Claire was all business, as usual. She arranged for the cremation and then tucked the box away in the attic. She got a promotion: Senior Vice President in Charge of Motivational Corporate Wall Communications. She was the youngest vice-president in the history of Motivate, Inc. She started coming home late, leaving early, using words like "results-based" and "value proposition." She put motivational posters up around the house, started leaving lists of things for me to do while she was at work, left *Smart Company* magazine open to articles about "Getting Back to Business" and "Four Steps to Spotless Credit."

She was making money. She bought a new XTerra and a living room suite. She put the old couch on the back patio. I sat out there and tried to turn my dark thoughts into dark novels. The couch still smelled like the dog.

By the time she sat down with that look in her eye, concerned and resolved and looking forward to getting it all over with, whatever had happened between us had been happening for a long time, gathering mass, each little thing curling around itself, becoming part of the big thing, the morass of history and now that was our relationship.

I was sitting outside on the couch. She put a towel over a cushion and sat down. "We have to talk," she said. She sat up, pushed out her boobs. This was her professional pose. "I don't think we want the same things anymore," she said.

I poked at the cuticle of my big toe.

"I want an exciting life with a good-looking group of successful friends. I want a faster, quieter car. I want vacations on white sand beaches. You just want to sit on the patio and write the first sentences to novels you'll never finish."

I looked up and even Claire could tell she'd crossed some sort of line.

"You just leave them there in that stupid yellow notebook," she said.

I picked something that felt and smelled like a tiny piece of cheese out of my toenail, flicked it out into the yard.

"And that about wraps it up," she said.

• • •

I sat on the patio and drank a bottle of wine, smoked a half-pack of Marlboro Reds while Claire and her sister, the sister's boyfriend and a suspiciously familiar guy in Dockers and hair product worked through the house. They whispered over whose books were whose, picked through the plates and bowls, cups, mugs, wine glasses, and silverware, examined the George Foreman grill and the fajita machine and the smoothie dispenser. They took down the motivational posters. The sister's boyfriend yanked "If you're not riding the wave of change…you'll find yourself beneath it" off the mantle and leaned it next to "Adversity does not build character…it reveals it."

Every now and then the sister or her boyfriend would stick their head out, slowly, with a careful knock on the screen door. "Is this yours?" they'd say, holding up a Dave Matthews CD or an Old Navy fleece.

"No," I'd answer, without looking, taking another drag on my smoke and staring at the back of the strip mall across the highway. "It's yours. It's all yours."

• • •

It wasn't a decision so much as a thing I just did. A day after Claire left, I was standing in the bathroom shaving my beard with the electric razor, naked and ready for my shower. I looked down. Suddenly, it all looked so messy – a hornet's nest of thick, bristly hair. There were random gray ones in there, brittle and ugly, sticking out at bad angles. My penis looked like a lost thing, like a hand reaching out of quicksand – desperate, small, and doomed.

I pulled the razor off my chin and drew a delicate line along the bottom of my scrotum. Buzzing on my balls, a thin, almost electric prick. Black squiggles on the white tub.

I ran a finger along the skin. Smooth. I tugged on the loose sack, examined my work. It was bald, coated with innocent

3

stubble like a baby chicken.

I lowered the setting and went back in.

. . .

Without Claire my time had no organization. I woke up when I woke up. I ate when I was hungry. I sat on the patio and wrote the first sentences to novels. Sometimes I wrote the second sentence, and for a few, a whole introductory paragraph. In my head, I composed masterworks, entire books full of darkness and angst, death and misunderstandings and The Human Condition.

Time went funny. Every night, Claire didn't come home. She didn't come home at seven and at eight and again at nine. She didn't go to sleep at eleven so she could wake up for Pilates at six, and I didn't follow. The dog didn't pant up to me, bowl in mouth, at five thirty, didn't need to go out first thing in the morning, three in the afternoon, nine at night.

I wrote the beginnings to stories and I went to bed at midnight, at six in the morning, seven at night. I ate cereal for dinner, hot dogs for breakfast, sunflower seeds at ten in the morning. I masturbated and I thought and I watched SUVs creep in and out of the mall parking lot.

I wondered what Claire was doing, when she would call, whether I really missed the motivational posters or had just gotten used to the clear images of streams and sunsets, yachts and skydivers and wide blue vistas.

. . .

The next time was more deliberate. Why have balls that are sleek

4

and new when there's still a tangle down there? I got out the razor and worked my way around the bottom of the shaft, disgusted by how far the hair was creeping up the penis itself.

Why didn't Claire ever say anything about this? She must have felt something sneaking in there, had to wonder what was this wiry brush between our naked bodies, this fly in our ointment.

I looked at it, a thin line of black sneaking halfway up the front of the shaft. I ran the razor toward the tip, watched the trail reduced to skin, pink and new and elegant.

• • •

I decided to drive until I ran out of gas. Then, I would make a home in the new place. I would invent myself all over again. I would call myself John Folsom, perhaps would speak with an accent. When my new friends asked about my past, I would become dark and quiet. "That's in the past," I'd say, squinting and emitting a faint but recognizable hint of violence.

I started by drinking a bottle and a half of wine, smoking a pack of cigarettes. Then I drove to the 7-11 and bought more cigarettes. I went back to the house and finished the second bottle of wine.

I started packing but I only had my small duffel bag and there were so many t-shirts—old Dead shirts, shirts with the names of bars that had long gone out of business, shirts from summer camp and high school and college. I piled them up, one on top of the other, and they reached to my crotch.

All of these t-shirts could not make the trip. They had the names of places I'd been, things I'd done. A careful observer—say, the beautiful but misunderstood French librarian in the small town where I would resettle, who would slowly yet inexorably find herself drawn to John Folsom—might start digging around, could actually reassemble my past based solely on these cotton articles of evidence.

I took the shirts out to the couch, arranged them in stacks. I got my matches, sat down, decided to smoke one more cigarette before torching it all—couch, shirts, dog smell, Claire smell, everything. I sat down. I was tired, drunk, maybe hungover. I closed my eyes.

I woke up the next day with the sun. I was still me. I was not John Folsom. I did not talk with an accent. I was no more dark and mysterious than the Spin Doctors tie-dye I'd used as a pillow.

• • •

The final shaving was easy—exciting, even. I bought a new razor and some lotion that promised to be extra soothing for sensitive faces.

I took my time. I brought some extra lamps into the bathroom, put on some Thelonius Monk. I bought a hand-mirror. I went slow, delicately clearing a path. Then I lathered up and shaved the whole thing again.

Everything felt different. My fingers and my sensitive parts were like old pals who were seeing each other in a completely different light. Even the most incidental, everyday contact was a revelation. Something as simple as a post-piss jiggle took on a whole new feeling.

I went through two bottles of Astroglide in that first week alone.

• • •

Claire called. The machine picked up and Claire's voice told her to leave a message.

"Let's talk," she said, "We have too much history to just stop like this. I miss, you know, the whole thing."

She hung up and I watched the phone for a long time. What would John Folsom do? John Folsom didn't talk about his past. John Folsom worked a blue collar job and kept his mouth shut. John Folsom didn't need some motivational executive with an excellent ass and an SUV full of memories to give his life meaning and order. He lived one day at a time. He appreciated the small pleasures in life—a fine cigarette, a smooth bourbon, a young librarian's tongue placed delicately but firmly on his smooth, hairless balls.

I hit delete, watched the red message light blink once and then resolve into a perfect zero.

• • •

The couch didn't smell like the dog anymore, just smelled like smoke and mildew and highway exhaust. I walked around the house until I got tired. I stared at my yellow notebook full of first sentences. I went into the bathroom, shaved my head, looked in the mirror, and then shaved my beard, too.

I sat on the couch and watched the mall parking lot. I was restless. I felt like doing something. But the money had run out. The car had no gas. My t-shirts were already arranged in chronological order.

I stared at my reflection in the bathroom mirror.

7

bare

The eyebrows are the hardest part. You'd think that once you stand in the shower holding a razor on your scrotum that it would be all downhill from there.

You would be wrong.

• • •

I was writing outside on the couch when the sliding glass door opened. Claire. "Let's get back together," she said.

"Hi," I said.

"What happened to you?" she said. She ran a hand over my bald head, fingered the place where my eyebrows had been. I closed my eyes. It felt good.

"It's a monk thing," I said. I tried to put some sarcasm in my voice but it just sounded whiny.

"You're trying to get back at me," she said. "I probably deserve that."

She sat down, put a hand on my leg. "Let's get back together," she said. For the first time, I could see little wrinkles starting up around her eyes. I stared at her hair. Jesus, it looked wild. She'd let it grow out and go curly. It looked like a hive, like anything could happen in there. I wondered what she'd been doing all this time, what happened to the Dockers-and-hair product guy, how she'd been spending her time, why I wasn't more angry, and what she was wearing under her dress pants. "You can't be ready to just throw away everything we had," she said. She pushed out her boobs. "What do you think?"

"I don't know," I said.

But I did know. I was out of money. I was tired. And Claire was so sure of herself. She had no doubt at all. It was easy to give in. Maybe I needed somebody to tell me what to do, to get me onto second sentences, full paragraphs, to outline the novel of my life.

"This will be good," she said.

I nodded and tried to convince myself that it was true. I felt like I was almost home after a long drive on unfamiliar freeways, looking forward to that final sleepy glide through my own neighborhood.

"So it's settled," she said.

• • •

Things were okay for awhile. There was food in the refrigerator, gas in the car. We went to bed at eleven and woke up at six. We went shopping at the mall. Claire helped me get my resume together. The county came and took the couch.

But things were getting itchy. Stubble. It looked even worse than the hair had, an aggressive stand of tiny hairs colonizing my groin. It looked like a strip mine where trees were coming back, malformed and wrong.

"Let it grow back, for God's sake," Claire said. We had just finished making love, and I was staring at the stubble.

"But don't you…" I started.

"It's too much upkeep," she said. "You're spending an hour a day shaving all this hair. That's time you could be looking for a job. Cleaning the house."

I stared at the stubble. It looked like the stalks of things. It looked like failure.

• • •

We slipped into our old routines. Claire came and went. She pored over motivational messaging sales charts, plans for motivational websites, text messaging services.

I ate breakfast when she left, lunch when she called to check on my job search, dinner an hour after she got home. I sat at the kitchen table and tried to turn my first sentences into first paragraphs, pages, chapters.

It never worked. I was writing backwards. Each paragraph was a tar pit that kept getting deeper, laden down with history, detail, motivation, entire generations of backstory, until I gave up and started over with a fresh, clean sheet.
Valentine's Day loomed. I had no money. I had nothing to offer.

Claire sent me a text message: "Passion: There are many things in life that will capture your eye, but very few will capture your heart."

I sent back my most recent first sentence: "On the second day of June, Phillip Oshkovaka put his gun and canteen in a backpack, wrote a suicide note composed of nothing but the lyrics to Pink Floyd's "Wish You Were Here," placed the note beneath the Christmas tree his mother tended year round in the living room, and slipped out of the house without a sound."

She shot back: "Believe and Succeed: What lies behind us and what lies before us are nothing compared to what lies within us."

I replied: "In every house there is a place where the mid-day sun alights for just a second, illuminating the surroundings, the dust bunnies and forgotten toys, the food scraps and bits of earth that have fallen off workboots, until they are as lit from within, glowing, touched by magic."

I watched the phone, waited for the little message *ding*. There it was: "Achievement: Unless you try to do something beyond what you have already mastered, you will never grow."

Holy shit, I thought, she's right.

• • •

She got home early. "Happy Valentine's Day," she said. She handed me a card. She'd drawn a big heart and handwritten: "Love: The greatest motivator of all."

We stood there for a moment. She shook her hair out of its ponytail. I led her into the bedroom. "Make yourself comfortable," I said. I went into the bathroom. When I walked out, I was naked.

"What the fuck is that?" she said.

I pulled on the pubic hair, which had come back in. "It's a heart," I said. "It's the shape of a heart."

"*That's* my Valentine's present?" she said. She got out of bed, started putting on her clothes. She stalked into the kitchen and poured a glass of wine. I followed. "Put on some clothes" she said. "That's disgusting." She opened her briefcase and pulled out a stack of papers.

I stood in the hallway. I looked at the heart. I had let it grow back for her. I had spent an hour with the razor, carving perfect lines, fighting the urge to keep on going, to shave the whole thing clean.

"I'm not looking at you until you put some clothes on," she said. "This obsession of yours is not productive."

What would John Folsom do? He would give her *that look*—quizzical, a little amused, a little dangerous.

I gave her *that look*.

11

"Are you having a stroke?" she said.

I walked into the bathroom and packed the razor and my toothbrush. I grabbed a handful of t-shirts and my yellow notebook. I pulled on a pair of jeans. I took the picture of the dog, stuffed it into my bag. I slipped out the back door and into the car. I started it up and drove, through the neighborhood and onto the beltway. I kept going. There was plenty of gas. John Folsom might speak with a German accent. Or Spanish. Russian.

No, I thought, finally. He would talk like me.

Jack Kerouac and
the Amazing MegaFlex

Mary stops when she hears the crowd noise. Dead tunes and bebop blast out of car speakers. Vendors shout *Hot dogs*! *Gooballs*! *Wheatgrass! Fair trade soy lattes!* Beneath it all, a bassline of exercise instructors shouting encouragement—*one two three four!*—thumps like a marching band over a distant hill. She sneaks a shot of bourbon, stuffs the flask back into her bag, and mutters into the tape recorder: "Mary Nichols, Entertainment Digest, Jack Kerouac interview." Her voice is scratchy from nicotine, or the lack of it, and her head is fuzzy and tight. Too much caffeine, she thinks. Poor hangover management. She lights a Camel. The cool scrape feels good in her lungs, settles down into her head as she threads her way through the crowd. She knows about these people, the beatniks, hippies, grad students, and, most recently, bodybuilders and fitness freaks who are drawn to the old house and the man who means something very different to all of them.

As they get closer, Mary can't help but feel the excitement of this day, the mystery of the announcement he's been planning for the past few months. The exact nature of this proclamation has been kept secret, even to the media, but everybody has a theory. He is, after all, so much to so many. The beatniks and hippies are hoping for a tour, one last Kesey-style trip on the road. The fitness people are expecting some new contraption, diet, or exercise program. There are even rumors that he will be announcing a run for office. But Mary has her own theory: he is writing again.

She gets closer and the crowd tightens. She can smell funnel cakes and coffee and pot. It is like a combination of tailgate party, Buddhist sangha, county fair, and workout session. To her left, a group does circuit training on the fitness machine that bears his name. To her right, bushy headed kids play hacky sack. Old men read copies of *On the Road* and *The Subterraneans,* their heads bowed, silently reciting passages as if in prayer. They have closed off the street, and a stage is assembled along the fenceline of his mother's house.

Mary pushes toward the security gate. Two men are sitting on the grass. They nudge one another and stand. Mary keeps her eyes down, reaches for her press pass.

"You gonna make contact?" the older guy asks. He's wearing a tie-dyed t-shirt, baggy shorts, and expensive sandals. His salt-and-pepper beard is spotted with Starbucks foam. In his hand is a copy of *Dharma Bums* and a *Wall Street Journal.*

"What would *he* want," says the other, a musclebound teenager in a too-small MegaFlex t-shirt, "with a fat-ass like this?"

Mary has dealt with fans before. "I'm with Entertainment Digest," she says. "Maybe I can get some quotes after the interview?"

They give her a wide berth and Mary flashes her pass at the guards, signs in, and walks toward the door. The house could use a coat of paint and its shutters hang limply, like neckties on old men. She reminds herself again that the Kerouac interview is a plum assignment—a last chance, one she no longer deserves.

Cassady was on this porch, Mary thinks. Allen Ginsberg knocked on this door. "I'm a professional," she says. "This is just another interview." Then she catches a glimpse through the smudged window and her heart flutters like a teenage girl at a Justin Timberlake concert.

She hears the scrape of a chair, dishes being placed onto a counter. Finally, he's there at the door and she sucks in her breath, too mortified at first to talk. But the face is friendly. The eyes are still that deep river brown—brooding is probably what she'll call them in the piece. The smile is genuine.

"Mary Nichols?" he says.

All she can think is, "Kerouac Kerouac Kerouac…"

"You *are* Mary?"

Be professional, she tells herself. There's no greater sin for an ED reporter. Untalented, you can get by. Unprofessional, you'll never make it.

"Nice to meet you," she says.

His grip is firm. Hers is slippery. He moves aside with a sweep of his well-muscled arm. The kitchen table is set for coffee and Mary drops into a chair, squeezing against the wall. The room is small and cramped, a museum piece of strawberry wallpaper, knick-knacks, and 1940s kitchen appliances. A window ledge is lined with Hummel dolls. The place smells of coffee and dust and cigarettes. Miles Davis wafts in from the living room. "Should I turn that down?" he says.

She remembers the Mötley Crüe interview, the recording ruined when Tommy Lee wouldn't turn off a Three Stooges movie in the background. "No, it's great," she says. "This is one

15

of my favorite albums." Good music to write to, she thinks. He is writing again. He has to be. The idea sends a little shimmer up her spine, makes her want to get home right away and work on her own manuscript.

He fixes coffee, careful to ask whether she wants sugar or cream, and then how many lumps of sugar. While his back is turned, Mary takes out the old copy of *On the Road* and then stuffs it back into the bag. The flask shines up at her. She pulls out the laptop. Professional.

His hands shake as he places orange coffee cups down on matching saucers. They sit for a moment in silence. Up close, the brown hair is dyed an unnatural deep mahogany. This is something she couldn't see from the commercials or the gauzy press photos. His face is tanned and deeply lined, the skin pulled tight across his skull, not an ounce of fat. She makes a mental note that there's a map analogy in there somewhere, highways and blue-routes crisscrossing the leathery skin. His teeth are an unearthly white, straight and large and perfectly shaped, like a row of gleaming tombstones. All those years on the road, all those books, and nobody said anything about brushing their teeth. None of them ever wrote a thing about flossing.

"Sorry about the house," he says. "We're expanding the place in Miami and this seemed like a good place to make the announcement."

"It's fine," she says. "This is interesting." She looks around, memorizing details. "Mamere's house."

He nods. Despite the hair and the teeth, he's still attractive. She matches up the old man in the shiny sweatsuit with the black and white pictures.

"What's that, an IBM? A Dell?" he asks, indicating the

16

computer.

"IBM. Just a little thing, only good for writing."

"Yep," he nods quickly. "Computers are fantastic, aren't they? They do so much. I use e-mail all the time, stay in touch with my business associates. And, hey, did you know I post on the MegaFlex discussion boards almost every day?"

"I heard that," she says. "I guess that makes sense. You know, computers would have made it a lot easier for you. Kind of like the modern equivalent of typing on telegraph paper."

He winces, looks out the window and takes a deep breath. "Let me be clear. This is an interview to talk about the announcement. The announcement is a new machine. I understand we've been secretive about that. Trademark issues." He talks slow, looks her straight in the eye, his hands laying flat on the table. "But I've been very clear that I didn't want to talk about all that…earlier stuff. If the publicity people didn't tell you, then that's our mistake and it will be fixed." She nods and he continues. "I made a name for myself and, well, it almost killed me. And it was mostly bullshit." He puts a hand over Mary's and squeezes too hard. "But now I'm in the best shape of my life, selling a fantastic product I believe in with all my heart. And I really don't want to drag out those old ghosts."

Of course, she knows all this, knows his entire history. The childhood in Lowell. Football at Columbia. Years of struggle and then the excitement of publishing *The Town and the City*. More years of obscurity. The cross-country trips with Cassady. Six years of rejection for *On the Road*, and then the trouble coming to terms with overnight success. The loss of Cassady. The alcoholism and the diabetic coma that almost killed him at the end of the Sixties. The public rift with Ginsberg over Vietnam.

The embarrassing magazine essays and disconnected talk show appearances. The "comeback" in the Eighties—guest spots on *The Love Boat* and *Cannonball Run Three*.

And, of course, she is here to talk about the latest incarnation, the unlikely resurrection of the old beat prince as infomercial king, endorser of Jack Kerouac's Amazing MegaFlex, pusher of MegaBars, MegaDrinks, and MegaMeals, Nike-endorsed fitness celebrity beamed into millions of homes each day through the miracle of cable television and the Internet.

"Okay Mary," he says, "let's talk about the product. Let's talk about how each and every Entertainment Digest reader can lose twenty pounds next month. How, in only fifteen minutes a day, man, they can be stronger, fitter, healthier, happier, and sexier. Isn't that more important than what a bunch of lunatics did so long ago, a bunch of alleycats, stalking into half-opened doorways, pawing after the moon…" He catches himself. "We were just fooling around. We wanted to be famous." He takes sip of coffee. "Anyway, today we're going to talk about the product. Jack Kerouac's Amazing MegaFlex. And nothing else."

She nods, thinking about the tattered copy of *On the Road* in the backpack, sitting side by side with her own half-finished manuscript.

"Absolutely," she says. Professional.

He hops up from the table and touches her arm. "Hey, let me show you something. See this sweatsuit? Made just for seniors. It's light, but not too light, keeps the warmth. Seniors, they lose body heat faster. Nike's the only company working for the active senior. Fastest growing segment of the physical fitness community." He's smiling, tugging on the sleeve of his jacket.

The fabric is shiny and smooth. "Yeah, nice," she says, thinking about the bottle in her bag. One more shot and this might seem a little less surreal.

"And it moves, too!" he shouts, running into the living room with loud, plodding steps that echo through the little house. He starts doing toe touches and jumping jacks, his body rotating fiercely, steadily, popping up and down like a piston, still talking all the while about Nike and seniors and proper stretching and fabric that breathes, but not too much.

He really does look amazing. Not an ounce of fat on him. Tall and straight. He moves to the stereo and takes off the Miles Davis, holds up a CD called *Amazing MegaFlex MegaDisco Remix Workout!* and smiles at her. "The new CD," he says, then pops it into the player. A pumped-up version of "I Will Survive" thumps through the little rooms of his mother's house. "Could be my theme song, don't you think?" he shouts.

Mary nods. Her stomach hurts. This is starting to feel like a mistake, a bad trip. She stumbles into the living room.

"Of course you've seen one of these before," he says, walking toward a familiar piece of equipment in the back of the room. It's Jack Kerouac's Amazing MegaFlex, the same one Mary's seen a million times on the infomercials and magazine advertisements.

"Everybody knows the MegaFlex, or at least I hope they do," he says, patting the machine like a favorite dog. "But I don't think you've ever seen one of these." He opens a small gym bag and pulls out a contraption that looks like an elaborate slingshot. He places it in the crook of his elbow and pulls back steadily. His biceps swell like cheeks filled with air, then deflate as he relaxes his arm. "Jack Kerouac's Amazing MegaFlex Travel Gym!" he says. "You can take this thing anywhere, man. It fits in a suitcase. It's crazy! Sixteen different exercises!"

He stands on it, sticks his foot into the sling, and pulls his heel up toward his buttocks. "They thought you could only do fifteen, but I just invented this one yesterday. Hey, you want a better butt, I'm telling you, Mary, this is it!"

Mary tries to look interested. She's starting to feel sick, tight-headed and claustrophobic. Her face is getting hot. Sweat drips down her armpits.

"This is the big announcement," he says. "Fitness for the masses. Anybody can afford this baby. Just five payments of $10.95!" He pushes the machine into Mary's hands. "It's yours. Use it. You'll like it. And if you have any trouble with the exercises, just give me a call or look at the website."

She holds the Amazing MegaFlex gingerly, like a mousetrap that could snap at any moment. He puts a clammy hand on her shoulder. Mary notices that his fingers are stained brown and wonders if the color is from nicotine or self-tanning lotion. "And I really do hope you understand that this," he points to the piece of equipment in her hand, "is the real story here." He pauses a beat. "So," he says, "the person from *Rolling Stone* is coming in soon…"

"Don't you ever miss it?" she asks. "The writing?"

He wipes sweat from his brow with a Nike towel. "The answer is no. No, I don't miss it. I don't miss being drunk or hungover all the time, walking around in a daze, sleeping on benches. I don't miss the loneliness of rejection or the circus of what they told me was success."

"But isn't this so…I don't know. I mean, all those people outside? What would Cassady think of all this?"

He snorts. "Cassady? You wanna know what Cassady would make of this? Cassady was incredible. He could've done so much. The brains, the energy, the charisma. The physical tools. He could've been anything he wanted. You know how Neal died? On the side of the tracks like a bum. He was forty-two years old. He could've been anything, and he died like a bum. So don't give me what about Cassady. Cassady's dead."

She knows she should stop now, get out while there's still time to salvage the article. Be professional. "But the writing, didn't it mean a little more than all of this, machines and commercials and money?"

"The writing? You think that was real?" His teeth flash white and the veins bulge in his neck.

She takes out her copy of *On the Road*. The flask falls out and she stuffs it back into the bag. "This got me through high school, through most of college. This is why I became a writer."

He shakes his head. "That's not real." He talks slowly, sadly, like a parent explaining the Easter Bunny. "Wanna see real? Feel this." He puts her hand over his bicep. It is hard and solid. "That's real," he says. "That's something I made." He points to the MegaFlex. "That's real. And it matters to millions of people who use Jack Kerouac's Amazing MegaFlex to make their lives better. To get stronger. Fitter. Healthier. Happier. And sexier!"

Mary shoves the book into her bag, shakes his hand one last time, and slinks toward the door.

"Hey," he catches her by the arm, "don't forget this." He shoves the Jack Kerouac Amazing MegaFlex Travel Gym into her bag. "You may want to try it sometime," he looks down at her hips. "Take something off that ass of yours."

• • •

After she finishes the story—one thousand words on Jack Kerouac and the Amazing MegaFlex—she relaxes at her desk with a glass of bourbon, a pack of Camels, the novel manuscript, and *On the Road*. She reads the opening line. "I first met Dean not long after my wife and I split up." Like an old friend, it's still there. It will always be there.

How can he say that's nothing?

She pulls out the Amazing MegaFlex Travel Gym and places it on the table. A grotesque little torture device. She fits it in her elbow and pulls back slowly. The MegaFlex wobbles and almost pops out of her hand. She lets her arm relax and then pulls back again. The machine offers just enough resistance. She is working, but not too hard to try it again. And then again. Ten repetitions and her arm starts to shake. She drops the MegaFlex on the table and feels the blood pumping through her bicep.

A silly little machine, anyway. She lights a Camel and takes another sip of Beam. She's short-winded and sweating. Her arm feels swollen and useful. She picks up the manuscript and her pen, reads a line, and then puts it back down again.

Ryan Seacrest is Famous

Burns wakes up with the feeling that something is wrong. He can feel it in his…not in his gut, somewhere deeper than that, more primal. He can feel it in his balls. He sits straight up. How many days now? A week, at least. His wife is sleeping. Early dawn light suffuses the room. What is it, he wonders, a bad dream? Déjà vu? And then it hits him again, like nine-hundred volts shot straight into his testicles, it snakes into his gut and up his spine until it fills his head like a migraine. Ryan Seacrest is famous. Burns is not.

This was not always the case. Not when they were both students at South Atlanta High School and then the University of Georgia. Then, Seacrest was a geek, a quiet misfit prone to wearing the wrong shirt, Madonna instead of Metallica, flimsy silk instead of more workmanlike flannel. He was a loser, an amusing afterthought, a nonfactor. Burns was the one with the garage band, the starting spot on the basketball team. The cute girlfriend who, in fact, now slumbers away her nights and days as his wife. Seacrest was like a character from one of those John Hughes movies, always trying too hard, wearing those old man hats, the plaid pants and the ruffled shirts and the baby blue shoes. Always with the too-thought-out wackiness, his persona copied whole from videos and bad sitcoms.

Burns walks into the bathroom. His knees ache. He wonders

if he's coming down with something. He leans over the toilet and hocks a ball of phlegm the color and shape of a Hershey's kiss. And then another. Have to stop smoking, he thinks.

Ryan Seacrest's image is too neutered and clean, too mall-glossy for cigarettes.

Maybe the smoking isn't all that bad.

"You okay?" his wife croaks from the bedroom.

He grunts in the way that means yes I am and go back to sleep.

Burns looks around the little bathroom. The tile needs to be replaced and the toilet leaks. The grout in the shower is the color of snot and the estimate his wife obtained for some kind of tub lining system is taped to the wall. Three grand for a tub liner. Burns will live with the grout.

A wave of nausea. Maybe this is a migraine. But every day for a week? It could be MS. Like that guy Carbonell from human resources. And Peggy Whatshername from accounting, with the cancer.

Ryan Seacrest looks fit and tan.

I would too, Burns thinks, if I had a personal trainer, a chef. Jesus Christ, a hair stylist. Nothing to do all day but work out and eat right.

His belly makes a gurgling noise and he feels the sickness coming. He leans over the toilet and waits for the release. His stomach twists, saliva bunches and he lets a long string fall into the water. Another wave and he kneels down, puts his hands on the porcelain. Flashes of college, partying too hard, a group of people behind him as he pukes, stands, then chugs another beer. High fives all around.

Ryan Seacrest was never invited to any of the cool college parties.

The only time Burns ever saw him was at the radio station. WGSU. His show, the "Metal Experience," was right before Seacrest's "Dancin' Tuesday Afternoon." Burns would see him waiting by the little entryway, a stack of albums at his feet, his hair teased to ape the swoops and waves of the latest dance band, glittery jacket reflecting the fluorescent light like a low-rent disco ball. Like people could see you when you were on the radio. Like anybody cared what kind of jacket you were wearing.

His stomach settles and Burns retreats from the toilet. He looks at his face in the mirror. Burns has become concerned about his skin. There are lines forming along his eyes, smile marks on his cheeks. They are light, but he can see them setting, like cracks in concrete.

From the TV glow and the glossy pages of *US weekly*, Ryan Seacrest's face looks smooth and unworried.

"Why all this concern, all this effort, over Ryan Seacrest?" It is the internal voice, his superego or conscience, whatever, the awareness he carries around like a backpack full of Bibles. Unfortunately, it speaks, has always spoken, in the voice of Colonel Klink from *Hogan's Heroes*. Burns is reflective, and he has been using, or hearing, or channeling this voice since he was a child. He wishes it wasn't Klink, but he could no more change this than the scars on his knees or the fillings in his teeth. "Is that what you wish?" Klink asks, "to be Ryan Seacrest?"

"Fuck no," Burns says.

"Are you okay?" his wife shouts.

He makes the grunting noise again.

"Talking to yourself," she says.

He moves into the bedroom and puts on his underwear, the suit pants and the dark socks. Just like a million other people, he thinks, strapping on a million suits, packing bags and briefcases, hurrying off to one place or another.

His wife slips into the bathroom, pats him on the shoulder as she passes.

Ryan Seacrest dresses like a teenager, in t-shirts that Burns doesn't even understand, jeans that flare out on the bottom, with white splotches on the thighs—the kind that make Burns blush when he tries them on in the department store.

It's the t-shirts that really get to him. Any t-shirt, he should at least be able understand.

"I believe somebody is becoming ob-*se-ess*-ed," Klink says. Anybody but Klink, Burns thinks, with his sing-songy diction, that goddam Nazi Freud accent. It's like being a character in a Kafka story written by daytime soap opera hacks. To be blessed with no self-awareness, now that would be a gift. Those people breeze through life with their perfectly coiffed hair and their easy manner and their lame, ghost-written jokes, bantering with the contestants and making out with Teri Hatcher and hosting New Year's Rockin' Eve, for god's sake.

"Those people?" Klink says, "or that person?"

His wife comes out of the bathroom. "Are you okay?" she says.

"Fine," he says.

"You look funny."

He considers telling her. This is, after all, the person who has been with him ever since high school, who would understand better than anybody exactly what he's going through. But she is already pulling the covers over her head.

Burns puts on his shirt and loops the tie tight around his neck. The nausea starts up again. He makes it to the bathroom and resumes his position above the toilet. Nothing. Just a sick twist in his gut. He is sweating and everything feels light.

"Interesting," Klink sings, "very interesting."

Burns lies down on the bath mat, enjoying the feel of the old tile on his legs. Cold. Everything else is hot.

Ryan Seacrest lives in California. It is four in the morning there. Ryan Seacrest is still asleep.

Burns stares at the bathroom light, concentrating on the white burn, allowing it to grow, occupy all of his vision. Finally he closes his eyes and the luminescent glob glows along his inner eye, a giant disco ball throbbing inside his head.

"Fuck," Burns says.

"What's going on?" his wife yells.

He grunts again. He watches the light. "Nothing," he says.

"God," she says.

Burns moves over to the toilet. He lowers his underwear and sits down. Things have not been regular since…fuck, he thinks, since college? That long? He ticks off the list of things he takes or uses for this issue: Metamucil, psyllium seed, Fibercon, bran cereal. He has stopped eating fried foods, spicy foods, lactose, red meat. He sits on the toilet and waits. Like everything else, he thinks, you never notice how easy it is until it isn't so easy anymore.

He pictures Ryan Seacrest sitting on a gold toilet, perched there for seconds while his bowels smoothly excrete yesterday's smoothies and grilled sea bass.

"Smoothies?" Klink says. "Sea bass?" There is a touch of amusement in Klink's voice.

Burns picks up a magazine. *In Touch*. He pages through a number of photographs of young actresses wearing evening gowns. Who are these people, he wonders, and when did I lose track of even who the hot chicks are? He keeps going. An heiress is in rehab. The son of some Greek shipping tycoon has broken up with one starlet and started in with another. These people all look so young. Their careless, confident faces remind him of yearbook photos.

There are six pictures of Burns in the South Atlanta High School yearbook. Two of Ryan Seacrest. He is not proud that he knows this number, but he does.

"*Ob-se-ess-ed*," Klinks says again.

Nothing is happening in his bowels, not even a stir. He continues paging through the magazine. And then there he is: Ryan Seacrest. He is standing on a boardwalk, wearing a backwards baseball cap, baggy shorts like a rapper, and a t-shirt with some kind of skull spaceship thing. He is kissing a woman Burns recognizes from some hospital show. The photos are blurry, but there is no question who it is and what they are doing.

"Now *there* is a *freulein* I'd like to get to know," Klink says. "If you know what I mean."

Burns sighs. It is true. The doctor is tall, blond, her legs are muscular and long. Even in the blurry paparazzi photos, she looks beautiful, impossibly unattainable.

In the radio station picture from the college yearbook, Ryan Seacrest sits on the floor. Burns, taller, more a mainstay of the station, stands in the back row. Seacrest is wearing parachute pants and a bow tie. He is perhaps wearing make-up, his cheeks blushing red, his lips pursed and slick.

And now Ryan Seacrest is kissing the doctor from the hospital show that Burns' wife watches. He wonders why she hasn't said anything, how she could keep something like this to herself. What is it they talk about now, anyway? The house. His job. Her sister's divorce. The possibility of children.

Children. Even thinking about it makes Burns feel like everything is closing up on him like a bear trap. He knows he should be excited about the possibility. It is, after all, what is expected, what is normal. But all he feels is a narrowing of horizons, like a bag has been placed over his head, his options locking in like train tracks, all straight ahead, no back and no turns and no straying from the path.

He drops the magazine and looks at himself in the mirror. He is squinting, his chin protruding like a fat man's. Next to the sink, an ovulation predictor test kit. Lately, Burns' wife has taken the whole thing to another level. There are gadgets, timers, tests, scheduled visits to various doctors.

Ryan Seacrest kisses the TV doctor with one hand on the woman's back, one hand holding his baseball cap. This reminds Burns of an old fashioned actress, pulling one foot off the ground, curling a high heel up toward the back of her thigh. Ryan Seacrest is a bachelor. Next week he will be in these same magazines, wearing some new, ponderous t-shirt, jeans that cost more than a tub liner, kissing some other woman—a newscaster, a make-up artist, the girl in the sitcom about the mobsters.

"Seriously," his wife yells. "Are you going to work or not?"

Burns sits on the toilet.

"I'm ovulating," she says.

"She is *ov-u-laaaaa-ting*," Klink says. Burns is sure he hears a giggle in Klink's voice.

He hangs his head. From this position, he can see the doctor kissing Ryan Seacrest. Her ass is perfect. She is young and famous in Hollywood. Her horizons are endless and she is kissing Ryan Seacrest.

29

Burns feels an erection growing. He handles himself, gently at first, then harder, up and down. He closes his eyes and he sees the doctor. She peels off her scrubs, wearing nothing but a thong. This thong thing is new. In Burns' day, you were lucky to encounter anything smaller, more revealing, than your own tighty-whiteys.

"You are so cool," the doctor tells him. She removes the thong. Burns is getting closer. She straddles him. And then they are on the boardwalk. Burns is kissing the doctor, one hand on her muscular back, one hand adjusting his baseball hat. As he finishes, he can almost smell the ocean, the funnel cakes drifting across the boardwalk, he can feel the silky cotton of his hundred dollar t-shirt, the doctor's hands on his sides.

Burns opens his eyes. He is on the toilet in his tiny bathroom. He is breathing heavily. He wipes himself off and drops the tissue into the wastebasket.

"My goodness," Klink says.

"I'm fucking ovulating," his wife says. "If you're not working then get in here."

Burns looks at his shrinking penis. It is small and spent. He can feel the sickness coming again. Ryan Seacrest puts one hand on the doctor's back, another on his baseball hat. Burns can smell the bathroom mildew, looks up to see the cracks in the ceiling, the little hairs that have gathered with dust along the walls.

"Ryan Seacrest," Klink says, "is famous."

On Sunday Will Be Clown

Clown Code of Ethics: Clown Commandment Number One

> *I will keep my acts, performance and behavior in
> good taste while I am in costume and makeup. I will
> remember at all times that I have been accepted as
> a member of the clown club only to provide others,
> principally children, with clean clown comedy
> entertainment. I will remember that a good clown
> entertains others by making fun of himself or herself
> and not at the expense or embarrassment of others.*

As soon as I see the sign I feel like putting my big red clown boot
up Ramon's ass. Just below the neon orange SMITTIES: ALL YOU
CARE TO EAT (AND MORE!) sign, he's lettered ON SUNDAY WILL BE
CLOWN. This is supposed to say SUNDAY! SHOOPY THE CLOWN
AND HIS FABULOUS ANTICS! JUGGLING! BALLOON ANIMALS! GAMES!
AND FUN!, as I specifically requested. ON SUNDAY WILL BE CLOWN.
Like every clown is exactly alike. Like "clown" is the same as
"moonbounce" or "fried clam platter," and nobody will notice if
Ramon pulls in that drunk Smiley the Clown from Harrisburg or

poor old Jokey the Clown from Williamsport, with his trick back and his colostomy bag. Surely, this is Ramon's way of sending a not-so-subtle message: "Fuck you, Shoopy. The girl is mine."

I park the wagon near the back entrance and do my breathing exercises. Be professional, I tell myself. Think about the children. I take the wedding band off my finger and put it into the glove compartment. Shoopy, my character, is definitely not married.

Plus, if Cindi saw me still wearing the thing, she'd shit.

I take out the photograph and the Seven Commandments. In the photo, Cindi and I smile through the mist, Niagara Falls rushing in the background. I stare for a minute, my eyes moving from Cindi to me to the pounding water behind us. We are young and without worry, and as usual the look on my face—a mixture of arrogance and happiness—makes me want to smack myself silly.

A pickup screeches to a stop, and a skinny man in greasy jeans and a western shirt leads a tiny girl toward the entrance.

I tuck the photo back into my wallet and read the Commandments, slow and methodical, my hand on the makeup kit like a pledge.

• • •

Clown Code of Ethics: Clown Commandment Number Two

I will learn to apply my makeup in a professional manner. I will provide my own costume. I will carry out my appearance and assignment for the entertainment of others and not for personal gain or personal publicity. I will always try to remain

dave housley

anonymous while in makeup and costume as a
clown, though there may be circumstances when it is
not reasonably possible to do so.

There's no mirror in the walk-in, where I'll have to change out of my jeans and into Shoopy's outfit, so I've learned to take care of the makeup in the parking lot. I empty the kit onto the front seat. First, I paint the area below and above my eyes with white. I outline a big white smile around my mouth. In the rear-view I can see people walking down the street, kids out on bikes or teenagers slumping toward the 7-11. Cars creep by and dogs bark.

I step out of the car, set the white with powder, then start painting the rest of the character's features. I use red greasepaint, then outline the whole thing in black. I stand in the parking lot and set everything again. The talcum burns in my nose. I let the smell settle, bask in it. It is not unlike the feeling one might get – one might once have gotten, I should say—after a line or two of cocaine. There is a rush, an initial stimulation in the epidermis that carries deeper almost immediately, and then it seeps, spreads, takes over the body.

And so I feel the arrival of Shoopy.

First, my feet start tapping. Next, I feel the sensation move up my spine, as if my limbs are getting lighter, filling with helium, moving up toward my head until, literally, my frown is turned upside down.

This is the first rush, getting into character.

Shoopy is a happy clown, what we in the trade call an Auguste. He is the kind of multipurpose clown who can fashion a balloon elephant, pull rabbits from his hat, perform an athletic yet comedic pratfall, and maybe give that shy, fat little kid enough

33

wonder to keep going another year. The kind of clown I could have used when I was a kid.

I lug the gym bag over to the loading dock. The door is locked, of course. I knock politely, my hand over my mouth, eyebrows raised as if to say, "Oops."

Nobody answers so I knock again, louder. I take out the clown boot and slam it against the door. *Chang chang chang!* On the other side, I swear I can hear giggling.

And so once again, the talent must enter through the main entrance.

In the parking lot, I check for Cindi's car. Ramon's Camaro is parked in the very back of the lot, sideways, taking up two spots. I wander in that direction, take a casual glance in the windows, my hands cupped to see through the dark tint. The floor of the passenger side is covered in Taco Bell wrappers and Diet Mr. Pibb cans. My heart sinks. Cindi has spent some time in that Camaro.

I make my way around the side of Smittie's. It's almost noon and the line coming out the front looks like a casting call for Wal-Mart plus-size models. These are heavy people, all-you-care-to-eat people, breakfast-bar, lunch-bar, dinner-bar, cut-your-own-bread, make-your-own-sundae kind of people. The women herd children one way or another. The men gather in tight little bunches, talking quietly, smoking cigarettes and looking nervous in their Sunday clothes.

I make my way inside. The line snakes from the cash register, through the hallway, and out the front door. A crowd is gathered near the backside of the all-you-care-to-eat bar, awaiting, no doubt, a replenishment of Smittie's famous fried macaroni-and-cheese. I try to look inconspicuous, but it is impossible. The face is set. Shoopy has arrived.

I'm still wearing jeans and the flannel shirt and I move quickly—"pardon me," "excuse me"—toward the front of the line.

"Mommy! Daddy!" A budding drama queen in a Barney jumper motions at me and starts wailing.

I make a vow that this is the last time I put on the makeup in the car.

I step toward the kitchen, keeping my head down. Already, I can sense the tension. It's going to be a tough crowd. The mothers are irritable, hungry, and tired, the kind of women who will not accept a balloon giraffe that looks more like a camel, even if you explain that a giraffe's back is actually more humplike than most people think, and the important thing anyway isn't the specifics of the anatomy, not even the length of the neck, really, but more the spirit of the giraffe. Is the end result more or less giraffe-like? Does the child find it to be giraffe-ish? These are the important questions.

But I've been doing this long enough to know that people aren't always concerned about the important questions.

"The hell is this?" Ramon asks. He motions to my jeans and flannel shirt. "You are Redneck the Clown?" His orange Smitties golf shirt is two sizes too small, accentuating his pumped up arms. His nametag brags "Manager." The mustache has never quite come in, a peachfuzz smear along his upper lip. He tries to affect a courtly manor and a sophisticated accent, the Ricardo Montalbon of Central Pennsylvania.

"You are late, my friend," he says. He smells of Newports and Old Spice: combustible. "Full house today, Geoff."

"It's Shoopy. And you were supposed to leave the back door open." I stand to my full height, suck in the belly and push out my chest.

35

"My good friend," he says. I grit my teeth and wish like hell he'd stop calling me that. "Believe me when I say that, most truly, I do not, could not, and will never, give a fuck." He crosses his arms, pushes out his biceps with the backs of his hands.

"Where shall I get dressed?"

"Same as usual," he says, then grabs an acne-ridden teenager carrying a vat of mashed potatoes toward the buffet. "Where you going with that?"

"Hey, the clown," the kid says. "I remember you."

I nod and bow.

"Please," Ramon says to the kid, "always with a scoop of butter."

"We need to talk about that sign," I say.

He grabs my arm and leads me to the walk-in freezer. I sit down on a box of frozen shrimp and he stands next to a wall of ice cream. "We need to talk about more than the sign," he says.

"You mustn't worry about the performance, if that's what it is. I am a professional. Despite our...situation."

"That's the thing," he says, "the situation." He looks at his reflection in a shiny box of frozen gravy. He chuckles to himself. "I don't know why I do this. I guess I feel as if it is, you know, the gentlemanly thing." He nods, convincing himself, satisfied with the level of Montalbon-iety he's inflecting into the scene. He reaches into his pocket and produces a ring. "Tonight, Cindi and I will become one," he says.

"You can't," I say. "We're still married."

"Separated," he says.

"It hasn't been that long."

"Long enough," he says. I stare at the fuzz above his lip. "There's more," he says.

36

"I can't hear anymore."

He stands erect, pushes out his pecs. "Then we're done," he says.

"I need to talk to her. Where is she?"

"We have a Cheez Whiz situation. She is rectifying." He puts a hand on my shoulder. "And please. Don't let this fuck up your performance."

• • •

Clown Code of Ethics: Clown Commandment Number Three

> *I will neither drink alcoholic beverages nor smoke*
> *while in makeup or clown costume. Also, I will*
> *not drink alcoholic beverages prior to any clown*
> *appearances. I will conduct myself as a gentleman/*
> *lady, never interfering with other acts, events,*
> *spectators, or individuals. I will not become involved*
> *in or tolerate sexual harassment or discrimination on*
> *the basis of race, color, religion, sex, national origin,*
> *age, disability or any protected status.*

I wait until I hear the air-suck *thwop* of the walk-in closing. My breath makes little puffs of fog in the cold air. I attach the rubber nose, open up the duffel bag, and hold the bottle of Rumplemintz. I twist the cap and take a slug. Warm.

"Congratulations," I say.

I put on the costume, do my voice exercises, work through three fingers and then a fist or two on the bottle. Every two or three minutes, Ramon bangs on the door and I do my best to ignore him. I check the magic tricks, run through the toe-touches and the stretching routine. I feel the alcohol running hot in my belly. I thrust open the freezer door and stride toward the dining room. Ramon tries to say something but I push past him.

Now, it is all about the children.

As I'm approaching the entrance, the swinging doors push open and Cindi emerges. She puts the carton of Cheez Whiz down and smiles. I freeze. She has let her hair grow and it falls in yellow bundles onto her shoulders. Her face looks like it's clearing up, her eyes sparkle green, the Smitties shirt hugs her body. My hearts sings, and then drops.

She smiles, a quick glimmer that looks more like a wince. Her eyes dart back and forth.

"How are you, Geoffrey?" she says.

I nod.

"We should talk," she says.

Ramon hurries into the kitchen. "This your act?" he says. "The clown will show the children how to get lucky with the ladies?"

"Ramon," Cindi says, "lay off."

"This is business," Ramon says. He sniffs at my face. "Your clown has locked himself in the walk-in."

"Again?" Cindi says. The disappointment in her eyes is like a croquet mallet to the groin.

"I'm fine," I say. "The show must go on."

"Cindi, my darling," Ramon says, "could you please check on the chicken corn soup?"

"Cindi," I say. But she is already bustling toward the back of the room. We both watch her Dockers retreating.

"Come," Ramon says. "Let's get this over with."

I follow him into the dining room and he rings the Smittie's

Cowbell. He turns to me and rolls his eyes.

"Ladies and gentlemen, boys and girls and children of all ages," he yells. He is turning up his accent, letting the syllables roll like bourbon tumbling over ice. "I present to you: Shoopy the Clown!"

• • •

Clown Code of Ethics: Clown Commandment Number Four

While on appearance in makeup and costume, I will carry out the directives of the producer or his designated deputies. I will abide by all performance rules without complaint in public.

I come out smiling, walking my clown walk, red boots swinging out front like flippers. "Hey-hi, Shoopy's coming by!" I sing. "Hey-ho, don't miss The Shoopy Show!"

Everything stops except the light tinkle of silverware and muzak. I pause, put my hand over my mouth, and make the Oops Face. I take two steps and hit the floor, tuck into a forward roll, switch into a back roll, and then spring to my feet, wobbling back and forth like the whole thing was an accident. I'm a big man, bigger than I would like, perhaps, but beneath that exterior my body still retains some of the muscle, the surety of foot that made me district runner-up in the two-hundred-meter dash senior year.

The Rumplemintz is starting to roam in and I wobble a little more than usual.

The kids laugh and the adults applaud. Cindi comes out of the kitchen carrying a vat of soup. I catch a smile in her eye as I pull out the tennis balls and start juggling. They soar up in different directions, and I scramble around the room, catching and then throwing each ball again, twirling and spinning. I narrowly miss the cut-your-own-bread bar, stuff a piece of cheesebread in my mouth as I catch the red ball and toss it back toward the center of the room. I snag the blue and the yellow ball on my way back, look around as if I've misplaced the red, and then open the front of my costume at the last minute. The red ball shoots into my shirt and I jump. The kids laugh deep belly-laughs, doubled over and redfaced. The adults clap and shake their heads.

I burp and catch a mouth full of Rumplemintz. Things are starting to move faster now, the audience a blurry patchwork. "Whoa," I say, making the Oops Face and steadying myself. I step toward the all-you-care-to-eat bar, duck into a forward roll and pop up onto my feet. I stick the landing but lose my balance. Falling. I reach for the bar and next thing I know I've got a forearm into the fried macaroni-and-cheese. My arm slips on the goop and I knock my head against the salad guard. I press a hand to my forehead and it comes away a sticky mixture of blood and processed cheese.

The crowd roars, parents and kids alike. In the corner, Ramon and Cindi are huddled. He whispers in her ear.

I stumble into the center of the room. On my forehead, blood and cheese, clammy and wet. I dry heave and catch the vomit in my mouth, swallow it back down, and dry heave again. The audience gives me a standing ovation and I bow, almost tumble again, but catch myself.

I slap my behind and produce the magic top hat. "Whowantshelpmagictrick?" I say.

Hands shoot up. I turn around, make an exaggerated circle of the room. Ramon and Cindi are watching me now. She looks worried. He is amused.

"Yousir!" I say. "Mygoodfriendmexico!"

Ramon smiles, strides to meet me. He makes a little bow and then jiggles his pecs, like a pair of dancing mice in his too-tight shirt. The kids laugh and the mothers ooh.

"I am from El Salvador, my good friend," he says.

"Southoftheborder!" I shout.

He gives me his look. "How may I be of service?" he says. He notches his voice an octave deeper, fully into Montalbon mode.

"Abracadabra," I say.

We have done this before and he is ready. He smiles again. "I believe what my friend is saying," he speaks to the crowd, "is that he will now make these keys disappear." He holds his key ring out, bows, and waits for applause.

"Inthere," I say, pointing to the jewelry box that protrudes from his jeans pocket.

"No no," he says.

"Justtheticket!" I say.

"Listen here," he whispers, "you had better back off and back off now, my drunken clown friend. Or your nose will look like this permanently."

"Whaddawesay!" I shout. The kids roar. The adults groan. The crowd is getting restless. A line has formed near the assemble-your-own-sundae bar. I look for Cindi, but she is gone.

"This had better be fast," Ramon says. He puts the box in my hand.

I pretend to drop it, snatch it out of midair. He wags a finger in my face. I turn toward the crowd and wink.

"Cadabra!" I shout, dropping the box into the magic hat. I tap the secret compartment and throw a handful of confetti. I hold the hat upside down, shake it, but the box does not come out. I make the Oops Face and throw another handful of confetti toward the audience.

"Thanks girls, boys! I say. "Shoopy Shoopy Shoopy the Clown!"

There's a nice round of applause and the quick scrape of chairs as they rush back toward the sundae bar.

I retreat into the kitchen.

Ramon taps me on the shoulder.

"Gimme," he says.

"Magic," I say.

I see him winding up and then the fist coming toward the big red nose. I make the Oops Face.

• • •

Clown Code of Ethics: Clown Commandment Number Five

I will remove my makeup and change into my street clothes as soon as possible following my appearance, so that I cannot be associated with any incident that may be detrimental to the good name of clowning. I will conduct myself as a gentleman/lady at all times.

I wake to the sound of garbage cans scraping along the kitchen floor. I am flat on my back on the couch in Ramon's office. The clown shoes are still on my feet. My makeup is caked on, plastered like a cheap Halloween mask. I open my mouth and can feel it cracking on my cheeks. The lights are blazing.

"Are you okay?" Cindi says.

"No," I say.

42

"Sure you are," she says. She smiles, puts a hand on my head. "You were sweating so much, I thought you might have a fever." Her hand feels nice on my forehead. "But I think it was just the suit."

"What happened?"

"It wasn't good." She leans forward. "You better give him that ring. He's pissed." She drops the top hat in my lap. The secret compartment is torn to shreds. "In your boot?" she says.

I nod.

"He couldn't get them off. Almost got the meat slicer in here, but I…"

"If I give it to him, he's going to give it to you," I say.

"Yes."

"Will you take it?"

She looks at the ceiling. "I don't know."

"We're still married," I say.

"Separated." She leans back and scrunches up her forehead in the way she does.

"We need to give it another chance," I say. "It'll be good this time."

"It'll be same as the rest of the times," she says. She looks tired. "Besides, Ramon got offered a job out near Pittsburgh, opening a new Smitties. He wants me to go with him."

"Cindi," I say.

"I have to get the Jell-O ready for tomorrow's lunch." She pushes open the door and pauses. "Give him back that ring," she says.

I stare at the lights. The door clicks shut.

• • •

Clown Code of Ethics: Clown Commandment Number Six

I will do my very best to maintain the best clown standards of makeup, costuming, properties, and comedy.

"Another," I say, sliding the empty shot glass across the bar. Ada pours from the bottle of Rumplemintz. I light another Winston. The door opens and Shambach comes waddling in. The smell of night air and baking bread wafts in with him.

Ada pulls a mug out of the freezer and starts pouring Yuengling. "Second shift?" she says.

"Just got done," he says. He points to me. "You?"

"First. Tomorrow," I say.

"The hell happened to your nose?" Shambach says. "Why you still wearing the clown stuff?" He sits down, moves the clown shoes over a few stools so he can rest his elbows on the sticky bar.

Ada swipes a Winston from my pack. "Can't you tell," she says to Shambach, "that we're still in the post-show come-down period here?"

"You got, like, white shit, man, all over your cheeks there," he says. He leans over and starts wiping at my ears. I can smell the fresh-bread stink you can never get out of your clothes after even five minutes at the Buttercrust plant. "This is new," he says, "drinking with a clown. Why don't you do something educational, maybe we can all get smarter here or something."

On the jukebox, Lynyrd Skynyrd is singing about Alabama.

"Smarter's not the idea," I say.

He looks at my suit. "Won't argue with that," he says.

44

"It's more like lighter, I guess. What you want is to kind of take the weight out of everything, give them a few minutes when they're too busy laughing at you to worry about anything else." I finish my drink, swish the peppermint liquid around in my mouth. "If you really want to know."

"I'll take your word for it," he says.

I light another cigarette. I'm going to have to dryclean the suit. A clown that smells like Ada's Bar is not a good clown. Probably run me twenty bucks, fifteen at the least.

"What's the latest on Cindi and the other guy?" Shambach says.

"Let's talk about something else," I say.

The song ends. Johnny Cash starts singing about a burning love.

"That's really all we talk about," Shambach says. He finishes his beer, rests the empty on the bar. Ada flips through the channels. "I seen that movie you told me about," Shambach says. "That *Lord of the Ring*."

"What'd you think?" I say.

"I thought elves was small," he says. "That whole thing with that one with the bow and arrow and he's the same size, bigger even, than them other ones. Didn't seem too realistic to me."

The door swings open and Shambach mutters "shit," moves two stools down. I take a deep breath, try to start the breathing exercises. The hand slaps my back.

"We have to talk, my good friend," Ramon says.

"You gotta stop calling me that," I say.

"This all has to stop," he says.

"Duh," I say.

"I need that ring back," he says. He reaches for my Winstons

45

and I put a hand over the pack. He drops a pack of Newports on the bar and smiles. "You are a complicated man, clown," he says. "Or should I say, you are a complicated clown, man."

I stub out the cigarette and put the clown boots back on the floor. "Either way pretty much works."

He laughs, too loud. "Ada, darling," he says. "Bourbon." His accent is deeper now and he has lost the fake courtliness. He is drunk.

"What's wrong with you?" I say.

"I have lost my engagement ring," he says, "and my girlfriend is not speaking to me because I punched her ex-husband."

"Not ex- yet," I say.

"I punched her ex-husband," he continues, "for stealing my ring and putting on a mess of a show in my restaurant."

I close my eyes and try to focus but it isn't working. I don't want to be here. I want to be back home, back with Cindi. I want a do-over. I need to start again. I need a transfusion. Like Superman, I need to fly around the earth so fast that it will turn things back to the way they should be.

"In addition," Ramon says, "I believe you may have violated some of your sacred commandments." There's a dare in his voice.

"How do you…" I start, and then realize the only way he would know about the Commandments. I put my hand in my pocket, loop my finger through my wedding band and the diamond ring. Ramon is right about one thing: this has to stop.

• • •

dave housley

Clown Code of Ethics: Clown Commandment Number Seven

I will appear in as many clown shows as I possibly can.

"This is stupid," Ramon says. He leans over and pokes me in the arm, wobbling slightly. I am on the ground in a hurdler's stretch. The night air feels good. The road is cold and empty, the storefronts are dark. The bank clock says midnight. I lean over, stretching the muscle, touch my forehead to my knee. This is the best I've felt since I started putting on the makeup. The Rumplemintz burns through my system like gasoline. I am loose, limber, and ready.

"This is silly," he says.

I pretend not to hear, switch legs, and lean as far as I can.

Fifty yards down the street, Shambach waves a bar towel. "Let's get this over with," he shouts. Headlights appear in the distance and Shambach mutters, moves out of the street.

Ramon feigns stretching. "Is this some type of clown code of honor?" he says. "Settle all disputes with a fifty-yard dash? Like a duel, but with large rubber shoes on your feet?"

"Something like that," I say. In truth, I have no idea why I need to settle it this way. Perhaps because I know I will lose a fight or an argument. Maybe I can't bear the pain of allowing Cindi to choose, of really knowing that she would pass me by, once and for all, for good.

The car gets closer. Ramon stands and waves. Cindi is driving his Camaro. She glides to a stop and gets out. "What's this?" she says.

Ramon shakes his head. "This is the idea of your clown. How we settle our differences."

She looks at me. I stand and wave to Shambach, put my head down. The rubber boots are tight on my feet.

"Ready...steady...go!" Shambach yells.

I put my head down and run as fast as I can. The shoes slip on the gravel at first but I adjust, pumping my knees high. My legs are loose and the night air is cool on my face. My lungs burn and it feels good. After the first few steps, I develop a rhythm. Momentum. The shoes act like springs, pushing me forward, faster, and I pump my arms to keep up. I lean forward, pushing as hard as I can. The rings are clutched in my hand. The diamond pushes into my palm. All I can hear is my own breath, my pulse pounding in my head.

I hit the finish line and Shambach whoops, waves the towel.

I glide to a stop, a sudden tightness in my chest. I turn around. Ramon and Cindi are huddled in the glow of the Camaro's lights. He kisses her on the forehead. She hugs him tight. He looks at me and shakes his head. Cindi punches him in the arm. Her blonde hair is frizzy and she glows like an angel in the headlights. She says something I can't hear. I realize I'm wheezing.

"What?" I shout.

The doors close and the Camaro backs up, does a careful three-point turn. I watch the lights moving down the street, red and then pink and then tiny dots and then they are gone. I take off the boots and walk back toward the bar. In my hand, the diamond feels worthless, like a trinket, like nothing at all.

Frog Prince II:
An Open Letter to the Princess

Dearest Princess,

First of all I would like to apologize for the regrettably public nature of this discourse. I'm afraid that your decision to proceed with the restraining order, and the recent decampment to Ibiza, as well as the alteration of your phone and pager numbers, the closure of your email accounts, and the revocation of my security clearances and passwords, has left me with no choice but to contact you in this most public manner.

It is with a heavy heart, then, that I thank the kind editors of *Us Weekly* for agreeing to print this letter, especially at a time when so much of our national attention is, quite naturally, focused on the trials and tribulations of Lindsey Lohan.

Unfortunately, public discourse is the only outlet left to me now, the only means by which I can communicate with you, my love, my one-time one and only, the woman who quite literally brought me renewed life and then took it all away.

But perhaps you have forgotten, dear Princess, the nature of our relationship. Perhaps our shared history has been melted from your brain by the searing and famous kisses of Mr. Wilmer Valderrama, who now occupies my space in your bed and, I am loathe to say, my place in your heart as well.

Princess, let me remind you: once upon a time, a prince was turned into a frog by an evil witch. The prince toiled in the paddies of his kingdom, a lowly amphibian—cold-blooded, web-footed, peer of the newt and the toad. He lived as a frog lives, imbibing insects, lolling about (quite literally) in the muddy bottom of the food chain.

And then—miracle upon miracles—he was kissed. Not by just anybody. He was kissed by a beautiful princess whose very touch carried the magical power of transmogrification.

Metamorphosis.

He was reborn. A prince again.

But he was a prince in a new kingdom, a new world, for time had not stopped during the prince's amphibious seclusion. No, time had rolled on. The witch's curse assured our lowly frog eternal life, for he did not age, even as the land around him changed. As village turned to city and city to suburb, he retreated further into the swamps, sheltered himself under paddies, learned to love the smell of grasshoppers in the morning, the busy churn of the swamp at night.

And time marched on.

Until the kiss.

And so our frog prince was reborn into an era of fabulous technological advancement. Where once there had been castles and fields, there were now skyscrapers and parking lots. The music of birds was replaced by car horns. Instead of stars in the night sky, he could see only smog. Where courtliness and the order of the knight once ruled the land, now there was capitalism.

The prince was a person out of time, a pantaloon-and-feather man in a baggy jeans and Kangol world.

But how I tried, my love! I threw myself into my new world.

You were smitten (perhaps as much, I realize now, with the unique power of your osculation as with the results); I was in love.

I learned everything: music, television, history, modern manners. From U2 to Jackie Chan. From *Lost* to *Road House* to the Wu Tang Clan, I studied night and day, filling all my gaps, making myself over in the image I saw in your eyes.

And for awhile, it was all worth it. Why? It was worth it for you! We were together. Finally, forever, everlasting.

And how I enjoyed the modern conveniences, the television and the microwave. Cell phones! Refrigeration! Burritos! We lounged in the most comfortable deck chairs, swam in water of crystalline chemical blue.

How we laughed at Paris and Nicole as they tried to live *The Simple Life*. How we danced to the rhythmic bounce of Beyonce and Jay-Z as we looked into one another's eyes and sang it over and over again: "Got me looking so crazy right now, your touch, got me hoping you'll page me right now, your kiss, got me hoping you'll save me right now…"

Your kiss. Indeed.

We were the brightest, the most beautiful. I exchanged my puffy shirt for Tommy Hilfiger and you signed the contract with Versace. Those were the days. Vacation with the Beckhams. The week on Clooney's boat. The house in Ibiza.

And now I cannot even think of these places. Like everything else, they are ruined forever by the mere thought of Antonio Banderas in that house, in our bed, doing god knows what.

But unfortunately, I do know, for I have seen the video.

I paid my $39.95 along with every other single, desperate man with a credit card and a cable modem and I watched my chaste, beautiful Princess, down on your glorious knees, legs akimbo and doublebacked with the Latin heartthrob.

Please, before you embarrass yourself further, my precious, do not protest.

I have heard your declarations of innocence, seen you on the *Oprah* show and watched your father's barristers doing their nightly spin on *Entertainment Tonight* and *Fox News*. But you forget, dear Princess. You forget that I am in a unique position to identify that little mole on your yogalates-enhanced behind, so despite the national outcry and the lawsuits and the grainy, amateur-video production values, I know it was you.

I knew that you were a "modern princess." As a human, of course, I did my homework, read the *Jane Magazine* features and the expose in the *Star*. I saw the websites and the Playboy spread. But you told me those days were behind you and I believed it all. And now to see you and Wilmer Valderrama splay-legged on the very comforter we received from none other than Queen Noor of Jordan...

Do you have any idea of the pain you've caused?

Did I ask to be kissed?

Did I ask, any more than Gregor Samsa, to be changed into this horrible creature who writes to you now, wretched in my longing, Gollum-ized in the national media?

Do you know what a joy it is to be a frog? To be concerned only with catching enough insects to get through the day?

There is a rhythm to swamp life that has gone missing in industrialized society, and we—no, *you*, with your Blackberry and your jet, your hair extensions and implants and botox injections— are none the better for it. Swamp life is a simple life. Predictable. Honorable. Of this, the joy of simple pleasures, you would know nothing.

There is perhaps a misconception about the catching of insects, a misunderstanding that it is a grinding, blue-collar job, long hours and little return. An emotionally stilted life.

Nothing could be further from the truth.

As a frog I was a hunter, a true part of my ecosystem. I ate, defecated, swam, and lived as one with my fellow beings. Rather than tread upon the grass or the bog, I lived in it. I was a part of the earth, connected to everything.

Was I a target for the turtle and the raccoon? Naturally. But I assure you, Princess, knowing now what I could never have known then, that I would take my chances with the raccoons and the bats and the fish – every time – rather than risk the vultures of Hollywood, London, Paris, or New York.

Before your kiss, I knew nothing of credit ratings. Car payments, interest rates, mortgages, lawyer fees. Now I am up to my eyeballs in creditors. The BMW has been repossessed. The Hummer is no longer in my control. My bank account has been closed. The AmEx card no longer carries its special magic. The men at the security gate prevent my access to your kingdom.

Can you imagine what life is like without these things?

As a man, it is pure agony. But as a frog, a different story.

And so now that you have left me, I in turn am leaving you, your world, all that you have come to represent. I return now to my beloved swamp. What's done is done. I am transformed in body, but not in spirit. I will lay down in the mud with my amphibian brothers and live that simple life again.

Goodbye, my Princess.

Ribbit,

The Frog Prince

Namaste, Bitches

We're sitting out by the pool, baking in our little network-issued bikinis, when Sir Geoffrey appears on the veranda. Emily and Martie sit up straight in their chaise lounges, push out their breasts. Martie pulls her top halfway down and gives herself another spray of oil; Emily throws down *Cosmo* and picks up a novel. I keep my head in the *International Herald-Tribune*.

Sir Geoffrey is dressed in his signature safari clothes – the same khaki vest, shorts, and pith helmet that twenty million Americans have come to expect every week. As usual, I look for security, half expecting a beefy line of Fox bouncers heading my way. As usual, I see only cameras and production assistants, waving ahead and trailing behind like tentacles, perfect moving parts of the organism that is the *Prince Charming II* show. Camera One follows as Sir Geoff's field boots echo off the tile. Camera Two walks along the edge of the veranda, filming the empty lounges with the name of each departed contestant written in sparkly cursive: Abby, Ally, Andi, Bai, Casey, Erin, Jacqui, Julia, Kimmy, Kelli, Melissa W, Melissa R, Mia, Paula, Shaniqua, Skylar, Tammy.

We are the final three. Emily, Martie, Himani. In a week, one of us will be engaged to a millionaire. "Prince Charming." Bruce. She will receive a diamond the size of a Skittle, a brand-new Ford minivan, and a year's supply of SlimLine FatBlocker III. These are the things that are guaranteed. What's not written is the rest of it, all the wild roaming possibility in a full fifteen minutes of American semi-celebrity: the cover of *In Touch*, morning coffee with Meredith and Matt, red carpets, open bars, five star hotels, *Maxim* and *Playboy* and paparazzi in the hedges.

For the losers, we are told there will be a twist, something a little different from what the runner-up got last season, which was a four-page in *Penthouse* and a one-week on *Hollywood Squares*.

Sir Geoffrey stops in front of me. He takes off the pith helmet and waits for the cameras to get into position. Martie rolls onto her stomach. Camera Three takes a few steps back, gets some footage of her shiny behind in the thong. Emily sighs, lets the novel drop into a pool of suntan oil, and stands. "I'm gonna take a dip," she says, her Texas accent dripping an extra layer it didn't have only a few weeks ago. Bruce is from Minnesota and everybody has noticed that the three remaining girls all have accents he might consider exotic. In this, of course, I am the undisputed leader—Nepal being decidedly more alien than Dallas or even New York.

Sir Geoffrey holds out a hand. "Princess, we have a call for you. I believe it is your father."

"Of course, Sir Geoff," I say, giving him my best J. Lo smile.

Inside the mansion, there's a flurry of activity. This is the moment they've been waiting for, when the Princess has to confront her royal family with the news that she's a participant on a seedy American television show. That within the next few days there is a thirty-three percent chance she will be married to a man they have never met, an American she has known for only four weeks. A white man who, if he does marry their daughter, will do so on national television in front of millions of depraved Western voyeurs.

Sir Geoffrey puts on headphones, gives me the thumbs-up. "Namaste," I say into the phone. There's a pause and for a second I wonder if it really is my father.

"Hello, daughter," says Bimal.

"Father, how did you get this number?" I say.

"Where are you?" Bimal says. I picture his apartment, the clothes strewn around, Taco Bell wrappers and computer boxes everywhere.

"I am in California. I am on an American television show, living in a house with two other girls. Before, there were twenty."

"What happen to the others? Have they been kill?" Bimal is pumping up his accent now, doing his impression. "Are you in danger, daughter?"

"I am not in danger. I am on television."

"A princess will not be living in this way!" he says. "You will come home. Marry as has been arrange."

"But father," I say. "I might…I might be in love."

Bimal slams down the phone. Sir Geoffrey pumps his fist.

I pretend to cry and run to the bedroom. The cameramen follow. I lay on the bed, moaning and keening, rubbing my eyes red. I look to Camera Two. "I love Bruce so much," I say. "I don't care if they have arranged a marriage. Bruce is my Prince Charming."

• • •

Transcript: Audition Tape
Himani Shrestha
Entry Number: 33422
Age: 22

Occupation: Student
Timecode: 00:00:00

Contestant: Hello, my name is Himani Shrestha. And I want very much to be a contestant on the new Prince Charming show. This is my cousin Bimal. (Gestures to camera). In Nepal, where I am from, it is not nice to talk about yourself, so I have ask Bimal to read me questions. So okay, go ahead?

Man: Tell a little about yourself.

Contestant: I am a student. Originally I am from Nepal. The Kathmandu Valley, so beautiful, where I have live until I come here for school.

Man: What about your parents?

Contestant: Hmmm…no, never mind. They are fine.

Man: What do they do?

Contestant: Never mind.

Man: Himani?

Contestant: My father is descended from our King Mahendra.

Man: So that makes you…

Contestant: Yes.

Man: What?

Contestant: A princess.

• • •

Bruce and Camera Three meet me at the door of his loaner mansion. "It's so nice to see you," he says, as if I'm a distant relative. Since he narrowed us down to three, he's gotten more formal, and the hungry, horny look has been replaced by a gleam of desperation that is almost endearing. I give him the smile that says "we're in this together" and squeeze his big sweaty hands.

I move in the door and the cameras rearrange themselves to accommodate me. Bruce looks like he's going to cry. His moony brown eyes water and he grits his teeth. His hair has been professionally mussed and he's wearing cargo pants and a zip-up sweater emblazoned with Old Navy labels.

"I thought. Since, you know. You haven't seen your family. For awhile," he says. "You'd maybe appreciate. Some. Home cooking."

I follow him into the kitchen and stop in my tracks. There's an older Nepali woman folding momo dumplings on the counter. She smiles but her eyes are cold.

I fold my hands together. "Namaste."

"Um-hmm," she says.

"So how you like it? I do good?" Bruce says. He grabs me around the waist, stares at my breasts, and leans in for a kiss.

I turn away, take his tongue on my cheek. "I am honored," I say, trying to force some water into my eyes, "to have been given such a gift." I bury my head in his shoulder.

We go into the dining room. A giant bowl of momos steams in the center of a ten-foot table. We sit at either end and eat in silence, the only sounds the grunts of the producers, the low hum of the cameras. The truth is, when we left Kathmandu I was twelve and already hated momos along with the air pollution, wild dogs, eighteenth century politics, and everything else about our third world ex-Shangri La.

Bruce looks at me expectantly. "This means so much to me," I say.

After dinner we move into the living room. Bruce leads me over to the couch. His hand crawls up my leg. The cameras move in for close-ups. In the kitchen, I hear dishes being scraped, water running.

"I think I must be getting home now."

"Princess," he says. "Prinnnnn-cesssss." I can smell the wine on him, his cologne like bathroom disinfectant and whiskey. He nibbles my ear. I lean into it, give him a little purr, and then kiss him slowly on the mouth. I part my lips for a moment and pull back. I squeeze his thigh and he wiggles. "I better go," I say. I fold my hands. "Namaste."

"Man oh man," he says. "Holy shit you turn me on."

• • •

Emily and Martie are smoking cigarettes on the front stairs when I get back. "Oh my god, I hope y'all just had a great date," Emily says. Martie snickers and coughs.

Namaste, bitches, I think. "It was very nice, thank you very much," I say, and scurry up to the room.

The network has removed all of the walls from the third floor and created some kind of teenage boy's vision of what a sorority would be like. There's a big sleeping area with ten queen-size bunk beds, all white lace and puffy down. The walls are painted bright pink, with a deeper, raw-meat colored accent on the moldings and ceiling. Cameras are tucked into each corner, and along the top of each bed. The whole place smells like new carpet and hairspray.

Against the back wall, a row of twenty mirrors, twenty stools, twenty hair dryers, curling irons, straighteners, assorted make-up and hair products. Along the top, the Prince Charming logo in neon and metal. A picture of Bruce smiling toothy, that horny gleam in his eye, is glued into the corner of each mirror. A giant neon sign runs the length of the wall above the mirrors, blinking a constant reminder that there is "Great Food and Fun at Friday's!"

I dress in the bathroom, put on the network-logo see-through nightie, and get into bed. Emily and Martie come in a few minutes later. They're still sharing a bunk, even though they could have spread out two weeks ago, when we were down to ten.

They giggle and chatter and finally I put in my earplugs, pull the blankets over my head. I try to let my mind go blank, but I can hear the whispers, can feel the empty space of the room, the absence of the others.

I wait for sleep to come. The neon sign pulses on off on. "Great Food and Fun at Friday's." Who would put this in a bedroom? But it's not a bedroom, I remind myself. It's a set. And it's not just a light. It is product placement.

• • •

Man: Which of your qualities are you most proud?

Contestant: That is a very hard question. As you know, in my country, this kind of talking about yourself is bad manners. But... if I had to, I would say I feel I am very honest person. So honesty. This is the one.

• • •

"We have a problem," the lawyer says. He runs a hand through his hair, slicked back with some kind of pomade that doesn't leave a streak when he wipes it on his suit. His foot is jacking up and down. Tap-tap-tap, tap-tap-tap. We're in the production room, the only part of the mansion that's not littered with cameras. This is how I know they're serious.

"What can it be, this problem?" I say. My heart pounds and my voice cracks.

"This is the thing: we can't find your father." He says it like a punch line. "The prince or king or whatever. We can't fucking find him at all." Tap-tap-tap.

"How embarrassing for you," I say.

"If we can't confirm you are who you say you are, it's gonna be pretty fucking embarrassing for everybody."

"But the background check…"

"Just to make sure you're not a porn star or a serial killer. This is a little more involved."

"May I ask where you looked?"

"Where'd we look? How about Nefuckingpal. The address you gave us in Kathmanfuckingdo."

"My family is in London," I say. "My father's business, it often takes him to Europe. In addition to the—well, you know—he owns several hotels."

"You can give us an address, a phone number?"

I write down a random number.

He stuffs it into his pocket, stares at me for a moment, his eyes brushing up my legs and lingering on my breasts. He shakes his head and leaves. I look again at the blank spaces where the cameras would be, and walk back into the mansion.

62

I'm doing yoga by the pool when the harp intro starts pumping through the in-house sound system. Then the electronic drums kick in. Finally the chorus and Mariah Carey screeching, "Prince Charming tonight…Prince Charming allright …"

"Sword ceremony!" Martie yells. She and Emily spring out of their chaise lounges for an oily hug. Camera Two moves in for a close-up. I towel off and follow them to the dressing room.

Network wardrobe is waiting to escort us into our princess costumes. Today they've gone theme. In place of the usual Cinderella outfit, each of us has a custom ensemble. Emily is a rhinestone cowgirl, glittering in her mini-dress and matching cowboy hat; Martie is a torch singer in a long mermaid gown, bright lipstick, and slutty pumps. I am, of course, an Asian princess. Somewhere they've found a red sari and matching chunri. Sir Geoff hands me a bridal bindi, tear-shaped and lined with fake diamonds and rubies.

"This is for a married woman," I say, handing it back.

"Just a prop." He winks and sticks the bindi on my forehead.

We follow Sir Geoffrey into the great room. They've placed torches and candles around the perimeter, and a layer of smoke pushes down from the ceiling. White hot lights loom like lunar modules. A shield with the Prince Charming logo is affixed to the wall, stressed with dents and fake sword marks that would look more authentically sixteenth-century if it didn't say "www. princecharmingtv.com" along the outer edge.

Bruce stands in the back of the room. He's dressed in jodhpurs and a puffy shirt unbuttoned to his naval. An upsetting thatch of hair is poised on his sternum. When he sees us, Bruce bolts

63

upright, wipes his eyes, and looks like he's going to throw up.

We walk slowly, smiling like nervous brides. Each of us stops on a silver X outlined in duct tape. Cameras move in for close-ups.

Bruce will not look at me. His eyes dart back and forth between Martie and Emily.

"Ladies," Sir Geoff says, "the time comes that our Prince Charming must make the penultimate decision. Tonight, two of you will be presented with the Sword of the Manor." He waits for imaginary applause. "And for one, there will be a twist!" Cameras are focused on each of us. My heartbeat quickens and I hear a sound like rushing water in my ears. "The one who is not presented with a sword tonight…will be flown immediately to the Island of Yap off the coast of the Federated States of Micronesia, where she will be one of two *un*lucky ladies on the cast of *Deserted Island: Island of Yap Castaway Princesses*! Coming soon! It truly is the ultimate…outdoor…catfight!"

Emily gasps and Martie whispers "whatthefuck."

"Following this, our Prince will have two days to choose the Princess of the Manor. The runner up will join our first Castaway Princess on the Island of Yap, where she will live with nothing but her own wits for the next two to eight weeks! And now," he steps back, "I give you…Prince Charming."

"How you doing?" Bruce says. "I hope you're all doing good." We nod, our desperate smiles flashing like raised hands. "I had a really neat time getting to know all of you. Really neat. So this isn't easy. Doing this," he says. "It's really. Hard." He shakes his head. "I'm not good at making speeches. So let me just do this." He picks up a sword. "Emily."

Emily squeaks once and wobbles in her cowboy boots. Martie

grits her teeth. My heart is pounding. Bruce kneels. "Would you accept this sword, Emily?"

"*Yesahwillthankyousir*," she takes the sword and hops back to her mark. Emily and Martie clench hands like Miss America contestants.

Bruce looks at me and his eyes dart back to Martie. He gulps and wipes a tear. "Himani," he says.

Martie faints. Emily and the crew crowd around her. The lawyer has appeared and he confers in a corner with Sir Geoff. A helicopter whirs outside. They strip Martie out of the lounge dress, put her in a jumpsuit with *Castaway Princesses* in big block letters.

I walk to Bruce and we stand. He hands me the sword and I take it.

• • •

Man: Tell us about your most embarrassing moment.

Contestant: In the tenth grade I ran for White Christmas Queen. I am living in U.S. for awhile and I think I am American. I think this is something I want to do, White Christmas Queen. So I make these posters: "Vote for Himani Shrestha—All-American Girl."

Man: Did you win?

Contestant: Did I win? I am not the All-American girl. Brenda Allbright won. She is blond. Her father owns the Taco Bell in Parkside Mall.

Man: That's not so embarrassing.

Contestant: I was in line. To vote. I am standing behind these two guys. Jocks. They point to my poster and laugh. They don't even have to say anything, it is so funny.

Man: Jeez Himani, that was like how long ago?

Contestant: I got out of line. I did not even vote. I tore down every poster. I thought, how stupid to think, All-American Girl. That anybody would go for that.

• • •

"So what's the story Princess?" We're back in the production room and the lawyer is leaning toward me, a courtroom smile on his face.

"The story?"

"We called that number. No sign of your father, the, uh, prince or king or 7-11 clerk or whatever. So why don't you just tell me what's the deal."

"May I see the number please?" He digs in a file and hands me the paper. "This is not the number," I say, "of course my father is not here."

"Come on, Himani."

"What?"

The lawyer sighs. I look to the corners. It feels weird without the cameras. I am having a déjà vu moment and realize that this feels exactly like when I stopped wearing the tilak on my forehead. You think you will be relieved, but the feeling is more an absence. Somehow without the thing you feel it more than you ever thought you could.

The door opens and Sir Geoff blows in. "How's it going?" he says.

The lawyer shakes his head.

Geoff kisses my hand and sits down. "Princess…Himani. You must understand that this is serious. On your tape, in your interview, you mentioned that you were descended from royalty. A great Nepali King." He looks at the file. "We took that, well, we ran with it. You are now, and will be for all of America, The Princess."

"Fuck," the lawyer says.

"We've been trying to get in touch with your family, confirm your lineage, and we can't do it. Now this puts us in an unenviable position."

"My father travels a great deal," I say. They both stare. I look to the corners again. So strange without the cameras. As if anything could happen. "I have not seen him since my…what was supposed to be my wedding day."

"Fucking A," the lawyer says.

"So not married?" Sir Geoff says.

"I did not even know the man. It was all my parents' doing."

"Well, that's not bad." He thinks for a minute. "But you are a princess? At least descended from royalty?"

In my head, Bimal's voice: "It will work. Just get into the finals and you'll already be famous."

I nod my head. "It is true."

• • •

Emily goes on a date with Bruce and I stay at home. They've

arranged for me to watch a "romantic" movie. *Titanic*. I fall asleep before they hit the ice.

I dream that I'm the Skipper and Bruce is Gilligan. We're trapped on a deserted island but he doesn't seem to care. I'm building a boat out of coconuts and Bruce walks up behind me, humps my leg like a German Shepherd.

"Don't you want to get out of here?" I say. "This is serious. Life or death."

"Have to get more bananas," he says. "More bananas really neat."

I wake up to the credits. Celine Dion wailing like a street cat. Emily is standing in the back of the room. "How was your date?" I ask.

She shakes her head, wipes a tear. "I love that movie," she says.

• • •

I'm reading the paper when I hear Sir Geoff's boots clacking on the tile. He strides in and kisses my hand. "I'm afraid there's a problem," he says.

"Where are the cameras?"

"Please. Come with me. Somebody is at the gate." He holds my elbow as we move down the stairs and I feel like a debutante about to make her debut. "This, uh, person," he says, "is claiming to be your father. He is producing a passport with the same last name as yours."

I picture Bimal, his hair whitened with flour, doing his impression for the guards. This was not part of the plan.

We go into the production room and Sir Geoff points at a monitor. On the screen, my father, hands restrained behind his back, glares at the camera. I suck in my breath, try to ignore the feeling that he can see me through the television. "Do you know this person?" Sir Geoff asks.

I watch father on the screen. If it wasn't for his flannel shirt and dirty trousers, his scruffy beard and hand-me-down eyeglasses, the dignity and fury on his face could pass for royalty.

"That is not my father." I say it as flat as I can, the way a princess would, like swatting a fly or turning away a beggar.

"Get him out of here," Geoff says into his walkie-talkie. Father is twisted away from the screen. Before he vanishes, something changes on his face, anger washing out into sadness.

"I'm so sorry," Sir Geoff says. His hand squeezes my thigh. "But this is the kind of thing you're going to have to get used to."

• • •

Man: So why do you want to be on the Prince Charming show?

Contestant: I think that this show, it symbolizes for me everything about America. You can be whatever you want to be. In my country, marriages are still arranged. The man and woman, they have never met. And then they are married. Even educated people. A woman in my position, I will never be able to choose. But here I can. And this is what I choose.

• • •

I'm nipping at my veggie-burger when Emily sits down at the table. She closes her eyes, mouths a prayer. "Amen," she says out loud. She stares at her salad. "Don't you just love him?" she says.

"I know it's weird. But don't you just love him?"

I stare at my unfinished plate.

"Did he tell you how he got that scar? Such a big goofball." She smiles and her eyes well up. "I just want Bruce to be happy, I really do."

"That is what we all want." I stand to go. She cries into her chicken Caesar. I rub her on the shoulder and she places a hand over mine. When I pull away, she clenches harder, just for a second, then lets me go.

I sneak into the bathroom and take the picture out of my purse: Bimal and I at ten, sitting on a fence outside Kathmandu, near where the tourists come to spin the prayer wheels at the Monkey Temple. Bimal is wearing a *Thriller* t-shirt; I am wearing a hand-me-down sari and shoes made from tire rubber. In the background, a group of backpackers, Americans or Germans, stands for a photo. They are young and bedraggled, careless and handsome in the way of Calvin Klein models. Bimal looks down at the street. I stare at the hikers. The expression on my little girl face is sad and knowing in a way that makes me embarrassed today.

I look to the cameras in the corner. Their presence, for just a moment, feels like an invasion. I slide the picture back and try to put it out of my mind.

• • •

The harp music starts soon after the helicopter comes back. They leave the motor running, whooshing white noise through the mansion. Mariah Carey warbles along with the harp and it sounds like an MTV production of *Apocalypse Now.*

70

They dress us in plain white gowns. Emily is given a Texas star necklace and I wear the bridal bindi. Sir Geoff leads us to the back lawn, where Bruce stands under a canopy strung with lights. He's wearing a white suit and white tie, like a steroid Gatsby. Next to him stands a priest.

Surrounding Bruce, rows and rows of people dressed all in white. White hats. White suits. White dresses, white pumps, white boas. Emily and I are given bouquets and veils. We walk like zombies toward Bruce and the crowd. When we get closer I realize the attendees are almost all celebrities of some mint or stature. The Black Eyed Peas. Pauly Shore. Kobe Bryant. A mousse-headed boy band takes up an entire table. Jack Osbourne whispers into Kathy Griffin's ear. Kato Kaelin stares pop-eyed and vacant.

Behind the crowd, the helicopter whirs like a giant vulture. "Castaway Princesses" is painted on the side.

"Ohmygodohmygod…" Emily whispers as we step down the aisle. I feel like I'm standing on a moving walkway, waiting for the disembodied voice to warn me about the ending coming soon.

We stop on our silver X's and Sir Geoff takes his spot at the lectern. "Dearly beloved. Ladies and gentlemen. Special guests, including the cast of *The Real World* and the one and only Mister Geraldo Rivera. We gather here today to witness a monumental event in reality television, the launch of a new series for Landscott Productions, and perhaps more importantly, a beautiful day for our Prince Charming and one lucky lady in waiting."

He waits for the applause. "Let me remind you that our winner will receive the Prince's hand in marriage,"—he nods to the priest—"and a ring from Kay Jewelers, as well as a brand new Ford minivan and a year's supply of SlimLine FatBlocker III. Our loser…whoever she may be…will become the second and last cast member of Landscott Productions' new show, *Castaway Princesses*! She will live in the wild, competing with the lovely Martie for food, lodging, and prizes. *Castaway Princesses*: it truly is the ultimate…outdoor…catfight!"

Applause again. I scan the crowd, settle on Kato Kaelin. He knocks his hands together like an organ grinder's monkey. He looks around, trying to gauge an appropriate time to stop.

"So without further adieu," Sir Geoff says, "let me introduce our one and only Prince Charming!"

Bruce nods at the priest and pulls out an index card. "How you doing? This was real tough. Tough decision," Bruce says. "I really like both of you. I think we got along good. Got along well. If I could choose both of you I would, but I can't." He takes a deep breath. "So I have to make a choice, and this is it."

My heart pounds. I wish I was back at home, watching this on television, making fun of the contestants and the third-rate celebrities.

Bruce swallows hard. "Himani," he says.

I walk to the stage. Bruce kneels. "Himani will you accept this sword?" He wobbles on his right knee, smiles up at me. There's a line of peachfuzz around his right ear, one curly hair sticking out. Suddenly, I feel sorry for him. He should have chosen Emily, who would be crying in an embrace with him right now. He should have chosen Martie, living off god knows what in the wilds of Yap.

The priest searches his script, shoots a look at Sir Geoff. The helicopter churns white noise.

I turn back to the crowd. They're all staring at me. What do they see? A Nepali princess about to take a fall? Another semi-celeb in the making, next month's *Stuff Magazine* cover girl, a ten-second blurb on *Entertainment Tonight*? All of them so expectant.

Watching. Again my eyes are drawn to Kato. He's dressed in a white suit with a bowtie, Bermuda shorts, and bare feet. He's wearing just a little too much make-up, clown blush dabbed on his cheeks, his empty eyes lined with black. He gives me the barest nod, not sure if I'm looking at him or scanning the crowd for somebody bigger, somebody with real celebrity, staying power.

Sir Geoff clears his throat. The priest mouths a silent prayer.

"Himani, will you accept this sword?" Bruce says it again. He drops his other knee and now he is kneeling as if in supplication. The crowd murmurs. One of the kids from *The Real World* lets out a scratchy laugh. I remember my father's face on the television monitor, that final look before he vanished offscreen.

"*Take it.*" Emily hisses. "*Take! It!*"

I open my mouth but nothing comes out. The priest is waiting, the helicopter whup-whup-whupping in the distance.

Sir Geoff whispers into his mouthpiece: "Keep rolling," he says.

Are You Street or Popcorn?

Are you street or popcorn? I trace it on the desk, my pencil barely touching the pressed wood surface. I try to stifle the half-smile turning up on the sides of my mouth, like I'm baring my teeth. Mr. Wilmer turns his back, working himself into his usual trigonometric frenzy at the blackboard. I steal a glance at my work. *Are you street or popcorn?* It has the right sound to it: edgy, challenging, vaguely pissed off, pretty much impossible to decipher.

I survey the room. Everybody is taking notes or daydreaming. Nobody pays any attention to me. Nobody ever does.

Since the article in the school paper, though, I have to be careful. People are looking for me. I see them searching their desks, hunting for the dense little messages that have been sprouting up like graffiti toadstools. Of course, the would-be Drudges of the *Shiksgrove Area High School Sentinel* got it all wrong. I think of these things as screeds. I just like the word. They called them "polemics" and tried to make some kind of sense of the whole thing. They blamed the usual suspects—disenfranchised youth, latchkey parenting, high school social isolation—called me an "anonymous questioning social commentator," a court jester for our central Pennsylvania school of jocks, cheerleaders, farmers, and burnouts.

If they ever find out it's just me, they're going to be really disappointed.

Are you street or popcorn? I darken the lines slowly, letting the pencil do the work. There are ten minutes left in third period. I watch Mr. Wilmer at the front of the class. The ass of his Dockers is smeared with chalk, and he wipes his hands there again as he contemplates out loud the mysteries of inverse functions.

Another one pops into my head: *Chalk ain't no measure of the man.*

I have no idea where this stuff comes from.

I look it over again. *Are you street or popcorn?* is etched in small, bold, block letters, like a prison tattoo. It looks right.

"Okay class," Wilmer says. "This is something we have to do because of these people who are writing on the desks like little fifth-graders." He pauses. "I need for you to all stand up, and I'm going to check if you've written anything on your desk during this class period." He folds his hands together like a Buddhist monk. "Again, I am sorry that I have to do this, but these people are vandalizing school property and Mr. Morgan is *pretty angry*." He practically sings this last part.

Wilmer raises his hands and we stand by our desks. This is it, I think. Sweat leaks down onto my sides and my face gets hot. My glasses fog and I grit my teeth. My mind is churning for an excuse. Can I say it was already there? Can I erase it in time?

This is the first time I've put a screed down on an assigned seat. I've been pretty careful so far, doing them on study hall desks, bathroom walls, cafeteria trays, all random, shared objects. "Never screed an assigned seat," I tell myself. It's the voice of Scotty from the original *Star Trek* in my mind. "Nev-ah ska-leeeed an assigned sheat!" he yells.

We're all standing, everybody rolling their eyes and making

semi-hushed, lame jokes. Wilmer meanders along the line of desks. He's about halfway through and everything is starting to cloud in my glasses.

Wilmer moves down the aisle next to mine and I know the jig is up. The girl next to me is weaving a little. I notice because she makes this little "oop" sound and steadies herself on the desk.

Maybe she's been screeding too. Since the article, I've seen some copycats. I'm not generally a fan of their work.

But this girl doesn't seem like the screeding type. Dorothea Quan is her name. She's quiet, a little mousy, keeps to herself. I notice that her glasses fogged, too. Wilmer walks by her desk and she falls, hits the floor with a thud.

Wilmer yells for somebody to call the school nurse. Everybody is laughing or yelling at other people to shut up, everything seems like it's in motion.

I sneak a look at Dorothea's desk. It's clean.

The nurse arrives with a stretcher. Dorothea Quan is awake, but just barely, opening and closing her eyes as she lies there on the stretcher and the nurse quizzes Wilmer about medications and the heat inside the room. The period bell rings in the middle of the whole thing and everybody walks around the stretcher as the nurse wheels Dorothea into the hallway.

I take the opportunity to erase the new screed, smearing a ball of spit onto the desk in a greasy smudge. I'm wiping my black thumb off onto my jeans as I move past the stretcher in the hall. Dorothea Quan leans over and catches my eye. She winks.

• • •

After school, she's waiting by my Chevette, puffing on one of those little cigars shaped like cigarettes.

"Cigarillo?" She pushes the pack in my direction.

I shake my head and she throws down her butt, grabs another one, and lights it with a silver Zippo.

"Virginia Woolf smoked these things," she says, exhaling with a little puff. "I'm pretty sure."

I have no idea what to say.

"We have to talk," she says, grinning in that way that tells you you're in on some kind of a private joke.

"Why'd you do that?" I say. "Today in class."

"I've been watching you," she says. "I'm interested." She opens the door and sits down in the passenger seat. I'm still standing outside. She waits, looking straight ahead and puffing on her little cigar.

Suddenly everything I've ever thought about Dorothea Quan, which to be honest, up until third period wasn't much at all, has completely changed. I don't know how to rectify this, to set my head straight again. This one bit of information has wedged itself into my gears and it's thrown off everything else.

She opens the door and leans across the wheel. "Come on."

I stand there, dumbstruck. This type of thing doesn't happen to me. Up until Jordan left, I really only had one friend. Now that he's gone, I don't have anybody.

So why is this girl smiling, sitting in my car and gesturing to the driver's seat?

"Get in the car," she says.

The Chevette's interior is thick with smoke but she doesn't seem to notice. It smells like cherries and burning leaves and Victoria's Secret. I roll down the window, then decide it's kind of a good smell and roll it back up again. I realize that I've had this car for four months and there's never been a girl in the passenger seat. Since Jordan moved, there hasn't been another person in here at all.

When we're five minutes away, she starts in with her story. She moved here from D.C. Her parents wanted a slower pace, the kind of life they read about in magazines and saw in catalogs. Dorothea does not want a slower pace. She's disgusted by Pennsylvania in general and Shiksgrove in particular. She calls everybody "yokels." She calls the town "Shitsgrove." She hates the fact that she can't get the Washington Post or the New York Times, that there's no Indian or Thai food, that there's really nothing to do around here at all.

"I mean, look at this shit," she says. "Cornfields." She waves her arms at the neat green rows that blur by on either side. "Cornfields!" She says it like it's the most ridiculous word in the world, like "platypus" or "spork" or "scrapple."

We drive by my house and I notice my father's car in the driveway. It's four thirty. Dinner in one hour.

"I was worried there wasn't going to be anybody here worth talking to," she says, "and then I started noticing these little phrases written around school." She looks at me meaningfully. "They're really good, you know."

"What do you mean?" I say, glancing sideways as she stretches her arms and yawns. I notice her breasts.

"I mean, they're perfect," she says. "The perfect commentary on this stupid little place and these closed-minded little people." She smiles. "It's just like a big 'up yours' and they all *almost* get it. I love it."

I take another look at Dorothea. She's wearing low-rider jeans and a black top, thick but stylish glasses, and big black boots with yellow stitching. She has a little button nose and big eyes. Her dark hair is cut close and messy, but done up in a little flip at the bottom, kind of like an Asian version of Mary Tyler Moore, way back when she was Dick Van Dyke's TV wife. And then there are the breasts. Again, a bit like the old, black-and-white Mary Tyler Moore.

"I knew from the moment I started seeing these things," she says, "that there was one person in this school worth talking to, and I was gonna find them."

"Well," I say, trying on a sincere but friendly look, "uh, yeah."

She squeezes my arm and I can feel an erection growing in my jeans. I try to fight it off. She's sitting sideways on the seat, facing me. She's not wearing her seatbelt. "Did you ever think it would be fun," she draws out the question, puts a hand on my knee, "to have a partner?"

• • •

Dorothea kisses like she's hungry, sucking at my lips, stuffing her tongue into my mouth like a dog going after a treat stuck under a sofa. She tastes earthy, like sweet corn and smoke. Her little hands are wrapped around my back and I can feel her breasts pushing up against my chest. I'm all fuzzy and it's hard to catch my breath. I can't believe this is happening to me. If this is what it feels like to be drunk, I can't wait to start drinking. Every inch of my body wants to get closer to her, but there's no closer to get.

Still, somewhere deep in the back of my mind, I know we made a mistake. It's stuck in my brain, that little pebble of guilt, and it's not going away, no matter how hard Dorothea presses into me. What we did was stupid, criminal even.

"What's wrong?" she asks.

"I don't know." I look at the pictures on the wall, framed portraits of Dorothea and her parents at various phases in their lives. The parents look the same in almost all the pictures—smiles, glasses, kind, uncertain eyes. But Dorothea is changing. I wonder if her parents can see it as clearly as I can. She's growing from an awkward kid, a smaller version of her mother, into this cute, smirking girl who looks like she knows something you don't.

"Oh, please," she says. "Isn't that a little *Brady Bunch*, getting weirded out by the fact that I have parents?"

"It's not that…" I let myself trail off.

Well, it is that, or at least that's a part of it. That and about a hundred other things, like the fact that I haven't really known this girl before today. Like the dinner my parents just started and the punishment I'll get for not telling them where I am.

Like the fact that we just hacked into the school website and posted screeds all over the place.

I rub the fog out of my glasses and check my watch. "I better get going."

She laughs. "Oh, come on. They won't be back for awhile."

"I really have to get going." I'm hot and confused. Part of me can't believe I'm running out of here. But I keep on picturing those screeds up on the school website. Just thinking about it makes my underarms sweat. This is not what I had in mind. This is pathological, this is real trouble, the kind of stuff that means you really *want* to get caught. I can hear the guidance counselors and police asking my parents if there was any trouble at home, if I was acting out, looking for help.

"I gotta go," I say, backing out the door. She's sitting on her father's desk. Her dark lipstick is smeared and her hair is rumpled.

I stumble out the door. "See you tomorrow," I shout, feeling free and relieved to get out on the street.

• • •

A week goes by and Dorothea takes control of what she calls The Operation. Her screeds tend to be literary quotes pulled out of context, so it's hard to tell what they mean or where they came from. She shows them to me before she puts them down, and I usually edit a bit, take out a lead-in or closing word to make it even more vague.

She puts them everywhere, on assigned seats and other people's lockers. She's hit the school website twice. She even scratched one onto Principle Morgan's Ford Escort: *Borne back ceaselessly into time.*

That was a pretty good one.

Something is building between us, but I'm not sure what it is. I can't tell if we're falling in love, or if we're just in cahoots. I'm not sure it feels like love. Dorothea is a little too pissed off for that. Instead of sharing our thoughts and experiences, going on dates, watching old movies together, and all the other stuff I see people do on TV, she mostly talks about how stupid everybody else is, about what a little shithole the town is, how bad the teachers are, how the people are all a bunch of inbred morons. How we're going to show them all with The Operation.

She's getting cuter every day, though, like one of those pictures hidden inside another picture, and once you see it you can't understand how it took you so long, and you can't see anything but that hidden picture, the little gem inside all the noise.

After two weeks, I send an email to Jordan: "I think I have a GIRLFRIEND."

He writes back, "very funny."

• • •

It's our one-month anniversary and I carry a gift around all day in my backpack. Finally, school is done and we're sitting in the Chevette. She's smoking a cigarillo and I'm writing all the screeds she laid down that day in our little notebook. We keep track now. That was one of the first changes she made.

I drop the present in her lap, kiss her on the cheek.

"What's this?" she says.

"A present. It's, uh, well, this is kind of stupid, I know, but it's like our one-month anniversary."

She laughs. "One-month anniversary?" She raises an eyebrow.

I grab the box out of her hand.

"Oh, come on," she says, "you can't do that. You can't give a girl a present then take it back."

"You can if she mocks you."

"Fair enough." She has that look in her eye, like some combination of a punchline and a dare. "But I have something for you, too. Not a *one-month anniversary* present or anything, but..." She reaches into her backpack, drops a book and a t-shirt in my lap. The book is called *The Motorcycle Diaries*, by Che Guevara. The t-shirt is red, with Guevara's face, fierce and handsome in outline, on the front.

"They made a book of that movie?" I say.

"That's not funny," she says.

"Well, thanks," I say.

I hand her the wrapped present and she opens it. "A necklace," she says. "A butterfly."

"It's stupid," I say, and I mean it. Suddenly, I realize what a little kid gift this is, how inappropriate for Dorothea and her plans, for The Operation. I look at the t-shirt. Che Guevara seems to agree with me.

"No," she says. "It's cute."

We sit in silence, watch the kids trickle into the parking lot.

"Okay," she says. "Back to The Operation. What did you do today?"

I realize that, for the first time in months, I haven't put anything down at all. "Nothing."

"Seriously, stop *pouting*. I'm sorry I laughed. Come on, what did you do today?"

I shake my head.

She stares. "What the hell?"

"I don't know, I just didn't. I had…" I pause, searching for a better excuse, but then the truth comes out. "I had school." I tear a piece of wrapping paper off the present and twirl it into a little ball.

"This is more important than that," she says, rubbing another cigarillo into my ashtray. "This is political."

I stare at the smoldering cigarillo. I clean out that ashtray every day, scraping the ugly brown butts into the Texaco garbage can. She never seems to notice that, every morning, the ashtray is clean.

"I just…" I start.

"If you're not going to take The Operation seriously anymore, I

84

don't think I can take you seriously," she says.

Suddenly, I'm exhausted. I feel weird and lightheaded, like my head is up on a pole, my neck stretched fifteen feet so I'm looking way down at everything, my arms too short to actually reach the ashtray or the steering wheel or even the cute little mole on Dorothea's thigh.

"And I thought tonight might be The Night," she sighs.

Everything comes back into focus. "What?" I say. "What did you say?"

"Nothing," she says, "I didn't say anything at all."

• • •

I send an email to Jordan: "This girlfriend thing is getting a little weird, man. Confuuuuusing. U out there?"

Nothing comes back.

• • •

"I'm getting bored," Dorothea says. "We just do the same stuff all the time." She untangles herself from my legs and rolls over on her back.

I am face-down in the green shag carpeting. My erection pushes at my khakis. I roll over, as usual, and stare at the fake wood paneling and the pictures on the wall. There's one I always wind up focusing on: Dorothea and her mother, only a couple of years ago, sitting on a blanket on a beach somewhere. Dorothea is just starting to develop breasts, little buds underneath her rose colored bathing suit. Her glasses are off and she's a little cross-eyed. She's happy, smiling a little kid's smile at her father, or whoever is taking the picture, and I imagine the goofy remark that made her laugh. I imagine the look she'd give you today if you tried to take that same picture, if you made that same stupid joke.

Dorothea sits up, tucks in her shirt, and puts her glasses back on. This is the signal that playtime is over. "Let's *do* something," she says.

"We were doing something."

She gives me that look.

"What do you want to do?" I say. We have this conversation all the time. It always ends with a screed in a dangerous place. It always ends with me fogging up my glasses, sweating through my shirt, sitting up in bed and wondering what the hell I've gotten myself into. Today, I saw two clean-cut guys in cheap suits coming out of Principal Morgan's office. Dorothea tried to convince me they were just photocopier repair guys, but they weren't carrying any tools.

"I don't know," she says, talking too softly, in a way that tells me she does know, and I am not going to like it. "I was thinking maybe we could take a trip over to school."

• • •

Today, we could pass through the scenes of our youth like travelers. We are burnt up by hard facts; like tradesmen we understand distinctions, and like butchers, necessities. We are no longer untroubled—we are indifferent. We are forlorn like children, and experienced like old men, we are crude and sorrowful and superficial—I believe we are lost.

The Erich Maria Remarque quote is stenciled across the shiny parquet floor in red letters. We're kneeling in the dark gymnasium, both of us holding flashlights, wearing black pants and shirts, like cartoon burglars. Grey light trickles in through the screened windows. The gym reeks of sweat and dust. The smell reminds me of my father's old Playboys, supposedly hidden in our shed, ripe with age and mildew. The bleachers are pushed back and the place feels big, exposed, like we're on a stage.

The stencil is a nice touch. Lately, we've gotten worried about handwriting.

"It's a little long," I whisper. My knees are sore and I'm nauseous from the paint fumes.

"Nope," she says in her normal voice. "We can't take anything out. It's too perfect."

"Isn't this a bit much? I mean, 'burnt up by hard facts,' 'we're like butchers.' They're gonna think this is some kind of manifesto."

"Isn't it?" she says. "It's about time you get some balls and—"

She stops. Keys jingle and boots scuffle up the back steps. Dorothea grabs the stencil and the spray paint and walks toward the front doors. I'm paralyzed. The footsteps are getting closer. She walks back, grabs me by the arm, and yanks me in the direction of the entrance. We slip out into the hall just as the back door opens and "Holy shit," escapes from the janitor's mouth.

We slip out the front door and make our way to the car. Sirens wail behind us, moving closer.

Two police cars barrel past the Chevette, sirens screaming, illuminating the tree-lined street and the neat houses. Lights come on in stages, moving up the street in the wake of the sirens. The cops take a left into the school parking lot.

My heart pumps crazy as the Chevette moves through the black fields and dim houses. We drive by my parent's house and I can see a light on in the kitchen. "This is the last time," I say. "It's getting out of control." She doesn't say anything, just puts her hand on my thigh and squeezes. In the rearview mirror, I swear I can see headlights back in the distance, following us all the way home.

• • •

I stay up most of the night, poking around online and looking for Jordan to come on instant messenger. I eat peanut butter crackers and drink too much soda, then I have to pee every fifteen minutes. Mom comes out and asks me what's wrong. I tell her I can't get to sleep and she waddles back toward her room.

I send Jordan a quick email: "Trouble in engeen loom, cap'n. Engage force field. Beam me up—now, you Klingon bastard." If nothing else, I'm sure the mixing of *Star Trek* metaphors will get him pissed enough to respond.

I try to read the book she's given me as homework: *The Motorcycle Diaries* by Che Guevara. I don't know what she thinks we have in common with this guy. We live in Central Pennsylvania. We are teenagers. We have curfews and bedtimes, yearbooks, SAT classes on Saturdays.

When I hear my father creak down the hall to take his second whiz of the night, I know it's almost morning. I'm just about to shut down the computer when an email dings into my box. Jordan.

"We have to talk," he writes. "I can't believe it. I mean, this is truly, really, agonizing. Like a knife in my heart. Like one of those supermofo ginsu knifes that cut through cans like butter. Right through the old ticker." A little dramatic, I think, but at

88

least I can talk to somebody about this now. I keep reading. "Joss Whedon has no TV show and William Shatner does?" he writes. "Commander of the Enterprise? On *Boston Legal*? Should I blow up Tinseltown? Advise immediately."

I close my eyes and fight the lump forming in my throat. I would love to worry about William Shatner right now. I stare at the screen until Mom calls me down to breakfast.

I'm going to have to figure this out myself.

• • •

I'm called to the office during homeroom announcements. I make my way down the hall, walking slow, wondering how long I'll be suspended and what my parents will say. I feel calm, almost relieved.

Principal Morgan is out and they tell me to go inside, he'll be there in a minute. The office is small and cramped, stuffed with little trophies and plaques that look like they came from a thrift store.

"Mr. Sherman," Morgan's voice booms behind me and I jump. "Scare you? Sorry about that." He sweeps his hands along the desk. "Let me check…" he says, smiling, acting jokey, but I can see the anger in his eyes. "It doesn't look like you've written anything on here."

"I didn't…" I start.

He holds up a hand to stop me. I notice he's wearing a big, red class ring. For a moment, I feel sorry for him. Still wearing the class ring. "Don't even start," he says. "We saw what you did this morning." His face is reddening and his fist is balled. "I just don't understand what this is about. You seem like a normal kid."

He stares and I can feel myself blushing. I'd really love to make it through one day, I think, without my glasses fogging up.

He gives me a cold stare. *Bleeeeeet!* The fire alarm goes off. Morgan looks at me, his face a combination of sadness and anger that says "you'll get yours," then he turns to the chaos unfolding in the halls. "Follow me," he yells above the whine, "We're not done."

I'm following Morgan out into the flood of kids happily making their way outside when a hand yanks me toward the lockers. Dorothea.

"You pulled the fire alarm?" I say, shouting over the wail.

She smiles. "We are such a great team."

She leads me out the back exit and up the little rise toward the football stadium. I reach out to hold her hand and she grabs my wrist. She's leaning into it, dragging me, walking as fast as her legs will carry us up the hill and through the swinging gates of the stadium.

Are you street or popcorn? is spelled out in giant letters on the football field. She's used red and blue spray paint, our school colors, in ten-foot, block letters, right across the fifty-yard line. A gas can sits on the question mark.

She's beaming, looking back and forth at me and the field. "Took me two hours last night," she says. I notice she's still wearing her burglar clothes from the night before. Her hands are covered in red and blue paint. "Come on," she says. I follow her onto the field. I smell the gas and my stomach turns. Fumes rise up from the neatly trimmed grass. The stands are empty, rising up on all sides. It's a perfect blue day.

She pulls out her Zippo and looks back at me. "You want to do the honors?" she says.

She throws me the lighter and I catch it.

"This is it," she says. "Everything we've been working for."

What am I doing here? I would give anything to be sitting in Wilmer's class right now, feeling bored and invisible, scratching something vague and meaningless into my desk. *Are you street or popcorn?*

"No it's not," I say. "It's not what I've been working for. It's bullshit. It was all bullshit all along. None of these things meant anything. It was just screeds, nonsense, fooling around."

"That's not true!" she says. Tears stream down her face but she's not wiping them off. I fight the urge to do it for her.

In the distance, sirens getting closer.

"And I thought I found the one person in this place who understood…" she trails off. She wipes her tears, rubs her eyes hard, and when she brings her hand back, her face is angry. "You're being so…so popcorn," she says.

Something slips in me and all of the sudden I feel weightless, relieved, for the first time in months I feel like me again. "I am popcorn! You're right. I've gone all *popcorn!*"

She pauses, stares me down. She leans forward like she's stepping into a wave. "We are burnt up by hard facts," she says. "You can't tell me that doesn't mean something to you."

I shout the first thing that comes to my mind: "Royale with cheese!"

"Like tradesmen we understand distinctions," she says. "And like butchers, necessities!"

"Space! The final frontier!" I shout. "Stacy's mom has got it going on!"

"This is serious," she says.

"These pretzels are making me thirsty! You bastard, you killed

91

Kenny!"

"I know what you're doing," she says. She taps a finger on my chest and the gas fumes push up into my nose. "You're afraid. Afraid to stand up, to make a difference." The stadium gates swing open and Morgan peeks around the corner.

"Hold on, you're right," I say. "Let me do it."

She shrinks back and I take the lighter. "I'm ready," she says. She wraps her arms around me and closes her eyes. Morgan and four cops jog onto the field with a lynch mob air of purpose. Dorothea's chest pushes into my belly, her hands balled into fists on my back. I take the lighter, toss it as far as I can, and hold her tight.

The Combat Photographer

The combat photographer needed health care. Not for a piece
of shrapnel in the knee or a stray bullet to the shoulder, not for
injuries sustained while running to the site of a car bomb, or
thrombosis or malaria or even food poisoning. There was a baby
on the way, and his wife was drawing the line.

I'm sick and tired of it, the combat photographer's wife said.
Gallivanting all over the place. Sudan. Afganistan. Iraq. It's one
thing to leave me for months at a time. It's another to leave your
child.

It's what I do, the combat photographer said. I'm a combat
photographer.

The combat photographer's wife tapped her foot and folded
her arms across her belly. She patted the bulge protectively. You
have three months, she said.

• • •

At the interview, the museum people were awed. This is amazing,
they said, flipping through the images of severed body parts,
burning twisted metal, mass burial sites. This is, the head
interviewer gulped and brushed his hand over a picture of a
Sudanese ten-year-old with a machine gun and a Chicago Bulls
t-shirt, this is courageous work.

the combat photographer

The combat photographer was used to this reaction. He nodded, made the face he made when people looked at his work—something between humility and gritty determination and recognition that yes, this was courageous work but still, somebody had to do it.

Are you sure you'll be okay working in a studio? they said. Will that be boring for you?

If I can thrive in that environment, he said, nodding at the portfolio and making the face he made when people looked at his work, I think I'll be okay in this one.

The negotiations took all of two minutes. The salary was slightly less than he had made as a freelancer, but of course there was a 401K, paid vacation, flex time, optional life insurance and disability and tuition reimbursement. There was health insurance.

• • •

The combat photographer marveled at how easy it could be to live as a normal person. Running water, hot meals, eight hours of sleep in a warm, comfortable bed. The combat photographer rode the subway, read the sports section, lingered over morning coffee in the photography studio while the museum filled with school groups, tourists, and families.

In the studio, he had absolute control. No wind, sun, monsoon rain. No bullets biting through the air. He took his time. He photographed the museum's natural wonders, exhibits that were being archived—the skulls of beaked whales, ghost orchids, stegosaurus bones.

His days passed with a reassuring regularity. He ate lunch at noon, took coffee at three, and left promptly at 5:30. He often lingered in the front of the museum on his way out, watching the children gape wide-mouthed at the museum's dinosaur displays.

He thought of the unborn child in his wife's expanding belly.

You were so right, he said to his wife.

She smiled and put her hand over his, then placed it on her stomach. Two months, she said.

• • •

The combat photographer was not used to being supervised.

Could you maybe move a little faster in the studio? his boss asked one day. Things are starting to back up a little bit. She waved her hand at the schedule, the line of boxes filled with things waiting to be photographed.

The combat photographer gave her the look he gave people when they were looking at his work.

Thanks so much, she said. We're just super-glad to have you on board.

• • •

The combat photographer began to wander. On a warm day he went for a walk and found himself at the Vietnam Veteran's Memorial. He took pictures of things left at the wall, homeless veterans in tattered wheelchairs, older men in sansabelt pants saluting the names of fallen comrades, their hands feeling the marble as if searching for a pulse.

For a few minutes his hands worked on their own, adjusting, focusing, loading another roll of film. And then he looked around. Teachers led school trips. German tourists ate ice cream sandwiches and perused USA Today. Joggers lumbered by. Women pushed strollers.

Six weeks, he thought, until the baby comes.

The combat photographer went back to work.

• • •

The combat photographer looked at himself in the mirror. He made the face that he made when people looked at his work. What he saw was a middle-aged man wincing and crinkling up his eyes.

• • •

The combat photographer found himself bypassing the subway for the four-mile walk home. He took the long way, through neighborhoods on the outer edge of gentrification. Occasionally, seemingly out of nowhere, he would find his heart quickening, the old adrenalin kick in his blood. He would pick up his pace, walking and then jogging down streets he had never seen before, like a dog drawn to an unseen mate in heat.

After a few minutes he would hear the sirens or would arrive at the accident scene to find two motorists in Dockers arguing over a fender bender, police filling out forms.

He would put away his camera and trudge homeward.

He tried not to think about what was happening to his body and mind, to his combat photographer's soul, but it was a long walk, and unlike similar walks he might have taken in Mogadishu or Kashmir, there was nothing to do but think.

• • •

I don't know if I can do this, the combat photographer told his wife. I'm a combat photographer.

You're going to be a father, she said, and gave him the look she gave him when the conversation was over, the look that said combat photographer, my ass.

• • •

The combat photographer started drifting into the front of the museum. He took photos of children staring at the stegosaurus, old women in wheelchairs, Japanese businessmen in their suits and shiny hair.

He spent more and more time in the front. Things were happening there, he knew, if you had the patience and the right kind of eye. He found unusual scenes—a young husband and wife arguing in a darkened corner, two school groups staring one another down, security bullying street people out the museum's giant doors.

• • •

The combat photographer had his three month review. His boss rifled through a pile of pictures he had taken in his first months. I think you need to spend just a little more time in the studio, she said, tapping the back of his hand with a manicured nail. Less time in the front.

The combat photographer nodded. He thought about giving her the look he gave people when they looked at his work. But then he looked at the photos laid out in front of him—dinosaur bones and flowers and fossils and bugs.

More time in the studio, he said, no problem.

• • •

The combat photographer waited for his cell phone to ring. The baby was two days overdue. He hunkered down in the studio, took what seemed like the same pictures he had been taking for three months.

He fought the urge to go to the front of the museum.

The phone rang. It's time, she said.

The combat photographer hurried into his office, gathered his things.

The fire alarm rang. He ran into the hall. People were frantic, crying, scurrying toward the back exits. He could hear pandemonium in the museum, sirens getting closer.

It's real, a security guard shouted. Fire in the archives.

The combat photographer walked back into his office. A calm settled over him. He looked at the cell phone, his packed bag. The sirens were just outside. The smoke was getting heavier.

The combat photographer grabbed his cameras and his camera bag. He opened the door and ran toward the fire.

Fight Club Club

When I get home, the couch and recliner are sitting out on the curb. Full-grain, caramel-colored leather, two years old. Pottery Barn. Sitting out on the curb.

I count the steps to the door—one two three four five six seven eight nine. I put my hand on the knob and then think, this is enough. One two three four five six seven steps back. I yank one end of the couch onto the lawn. The briefcase falls off my shoulder and a pile of monographs spills onto the grass. From the house, I can hear the sound of the movie, Charles and James shouting along with Brad Pitt: "The second rule of Fight Club is you don't talk about Fight Club."

Neighbor Bill gets out of his car, briefcase and lunch bag in hand. Good old Bill. Suburban, reliable, workaday Bill. He waves, nods, then scuttles into his colonial. Since Charles got fired and this whole thing started, the neighbors have been a little skittish.

Inside, smoke is everywhere. Miller High Life bottles litter the coffee table and floor. Charles and James and the fat neighbor kid they call Lumpy, who's back from college for the summer and doesn't seem to be working either, are sitting on lawn chairs in a semi-circle around the TV and the bong. Each of them has a Taco Bell bag resting on his belly; various chili cheese products are scattered around half-eaten. Charles has a cigarette in one hand

and a Beef Burrito Supreme in the other. The remote is balanced on his knee.

I close the door and lock it behind me. I turn the living room lights on, then off, then on again. "Dude," James says, blinking at the light, "do you really have to do that?" I check to make sure the door is locked.

"Why are the couches on the lawn?" I say.

Charles keeps his eyes on the movie. "You get that door locked?" His pajamas are covered with little pineapples and tiki huts. His shoulder-length hair has gray streaks around the temples that would look distinguished if he was still getting it cut at Christophe in downtown D.C. He holds a hand back for a high-five and I walk past him to the magazines, which are spread out over the floor, in no order at all. I know they do this just to get to me, but I pick them up and arrange them anyway, chronological order, based on when they were delivered, not when they say they were published. I keep my head down, ignore the giggles from James and Lumpy. As if I had a choice.

I go into the dining room. Lights on, off, on. I drop my bag into the space where the table used to be. I glare at Charles, pick the bag off the dirty carpet.

I go into my room and set up my work, *The Chicago Manual of Style* to the right of the computer, tonight's monographs to the left. Then I go outside and pull the mail out of the box. I arrange it into four stacks: me, Charles, James, and Mr. David Kingman, the fake name that Charles uses to subscribe to magazines and music clubs. Mr. David Kingman is getting some strange mail lately: weapons catalogs, martial arts supply, NRA membership, mail order chemicals. Mine are all bills and junkmail. Student loan, car loan, credit card, cellphone, two letters from the insurance company. I feel the black crawling up the back of my neck.

I check the lock again and Charles turns up the volume. "Maybe you better watch this," he says. Onscreen, Brad Pitt is getting beat up by some fat old man. Pitt keeps on asking for more, getting abused, pulverized. Finally, he pins the guy, shakes his head, spurting blood all over until the old man freaks out, retreats up the stairs. James laughs and sneaks a glance at me. His long blond hair is tucked behind his ears and he wears flowered surf shorts. He's been gaining weight since he moved in, the beginnings of a double-chin swelling beneath his jaw.

The truth is we're getting too old for this, sitting around and getting high, watching the same movie over and over. We should be getting married, having kids, putting money into retirement or college tuition funds. We were headed that way, right on schedule, with our grown-up furniture, real jobs, our love handles and serious girlfriends.

But bad things always happen in threes: Charles got fired, James moved in, I got in the accident. It seemed like, as slowly as the whole thing had built—relationships, jobs, responsibility—it was over in a flash. We were back to being twelve again, a bunch of guys goofing around, drinking too much and hitting each other in the nuts.

And then Charles found this goddam movie.

He hits rewind. Moving backwards, Brad Pitt gets increasingly better looking, the old guy pulling his hands away as if he's removing the cuts and bruises, healing the Hollywood hunk of leprosy, or some other disease that makes you ugly. Finally, Pitt is standing in front of the group again, all of them young and pretty, stitched and bruised, trendy in their Seventies vintage clothing.

"The first rule of Fight Club," Pitt says, "is you don't talk about Fight Club."

"Why are the couches on the lawn?" I say.

"Eventually, the things you own come to own you," Charles says. He's even trying to speak like Brad Pitt, over-pronouncing everything, rolling his Ls off the roof of his mouth.

"It's a movie." I say it slow, looking at the carpet.

"I know it's a movie," Charles says. He starts packing the bong, pulling pot out of a Ziploc bag and dropping the stems onto the carpet. "But it deals with real shit. Not the bullshit you're all worked up about." He lights the bong and takes a deep draw.

I check the lock on the door, then move into the kitchen to make sure the oven is off.

"Have you ever watched this movie?" Charles yells. "I mean, like, close? That fight stuff is just the beginning. And by the way, the *neat thing* is getting worse, man."

I know this is true, but I can't stop. I've always had to do certain things—wash my hands, check the locks, count my steps, turn the lights on off on—but since the accident, it's getting worse. Like my brain has hiccups. How can I stop it? Hold my breath?

"Look," Charles says. "Just watch the movie once, all the way through." James and Lumpy nod. "Have you even seen the Project Mayhem part of this movie? It's about, like, anarchy." He chomps the burrito and rust-colored goop dribbles onto his belly. "Besides," he says, "I wasn't the one took a bunch of Percocets then tried to drive home from work. I'm not your shitty insurance company or that bitch you crippled up."

"I didn't—"

"Only after disaster can we be resurrected."

"Is that from the movie?" I say. But he's not listening, he's watching Brad Pitt and Ed Norton stealing human fat from a liposuction facility. I stand there, trying to think of something to say. Part of me wants to knock his nose into the back of his head; part of me wants to lie down and sleep until it's all over. Onscreen, Brad Pitt teaches Ed Norton how to make soap. Both of them have black eyes.

I reheat some pasta then go into my room and edit monographs. Around nine, I hear Charles go up the steps. The water runs from upstairs, and he stomps back down again. The front door opens and closes. "Project Mayhem!" Lumpy yells. The BMW turns over.

I think about going in there and stealing the *Fight Club* DVD, hiding the pot, changing the locks. I think about cleaning the stems and beer spots off the carpet.

I take out the bottle and count them again. One two three four five…thirty Percocets. Ten will require a trip to the emergency room. Fifteen and it would get a little dicey. With my body weight, twenty would pretty much do the trick. I count out twenty and hold them in my hand. I take one, and listen to the rest tick back into the bottle.

I turn my Sleep Machine up as loud as it will go and try to lose myself in the white noise.

• • •

I grab the newspaper and drop it into my Civic. The couches are gone. I picture a family of Salvadoran immigrants relaxing on the supple leather, laughing at the crazy gringos. Somebody is picking these things off the curb and moving them into an apartment somewhere, someplace not far but not too close either, away from the clean colonials of our upscale neighborhood, the good schools, the Whole Foods, and the Starbucks. Somewhere, our living room is resurrected.

I would save them, each piece, rescue the whole house and bring it back. If only I could afford my own place. And if only they were my things to begin with. But they were Charles's, paid for with a squiggled signature on a trust fund check. The house is his, too, or his father's, anyway. Around the time this whole thing started, when he got fired and James moved up from Ocean City, Charles stopped making me pay rent, called it a hassle to deposit the checks and said if I couldn't pay in cash, don't worry about it anymore.

I check both ways, wave to Neighbor Betsy, reaching low to grab the newspaper in her purple bathrobe, and pull out slow. At the intersection of Richmond and Bradley, I toggle my head between both lanes and my rearview mirror. I need to make a left, get to Connecticut Avenue, and take another left. A Lincoln Navigator pulls up behind me and my face starts to get hot. There's no break in traffic. I keep checking, right left right left right. Nothing. The Lincoln toots his horn. In the rearview, I see gray hair and tapping fingers.

The accident started just like this. I took a couple of pills. I got stuck at an intersection with some beeping executive behind me, pulled out too soon and the next thing I know I'm standing in the middle of the street, bawling and shouting "I'm sorry I'm sorry I'm sorry" while the jaws of life cut into a brand new Chevy Suburban. The lawyer tells me that wasn't the best way to handle the situation, in terms of liability. The court date is in one month.

Another toot from the Lincoln. Sweat rolls down my sides.

Right left right left right. Nothing. The Navigator holds his hand out the window in a question. He's older. Gray hair, blue suit, red tie. I pull over as far as I can and wave him along. When he passes, I pretend to be getting something out of my bag.

I take the back way to work, pull in twenty minutes late with my shirt soaking wet. A cool wave of air conditioning hits me as soon as the elevator opens. Counting the steps to my office, my heartbeat slows, blood drains from my face. The American Pharmaceutical Information Center is my paradise. I am appreciated here. I am left alone. Here, everything happens as it should, each day almost exactly like the ones that have gone before, tomorrow a clean carbon copy of today.

I turn on my lights and check the in-box. I put the *Chicago Manual of Style* to the right of the computer. I sit back and relax. For the first time this morning, it feels like I can breathe.

• • •

When I get home, two guys in Jiffy Lube coveralls are pushing the entertainment center onto the top of a Geo Metro. "Escuse me?" the taller one says. His accent is Russian. "Hesh" is stitched onto his chest. "Can you give hand?" I walk back to the Metro, placing my feet carefully, retracing my steps. This way, I can start up again at the sixth step. It will still count.

Hesh indicates that I should hold the back of the entertainment center. I manage to keep it up long enough for him to get a roll of duct tape around the other side. "That's gonna ruin it," I say, indicating a spot where tape is plastered against the mahogany.

He shrugs and pats me on the shoulder, a little too hard.

"Thanks, man," he says. The other guy laughs. His chest says "Barney." They get into the Geo and drive off.

Six seven eight nine. The stink hits me the minute I get in the door. The house smells like chemicals, like a sewer in Chernobyl, a million Easter eggs sitting in their stain. I pull my shirt up over my mouth. I turn the lights on off on. "Joey's home," Charles yells from the kitchen. I put the magazines in a neat stack. Bile burns in my throat. I check the lock on the front door, drop my bag into my room, then go get the mail. I almost throw up on the pile of Mr. David Kingman. Finally, I make it into the kitchen. Charles is dressed in duck boots and boxers.

"Joe-ay," he says. "Welcome to the par-tay. This," he holds his arms out, "is the Wildwood Road Soap Company." James gives me the thumbs up. Him and another guy—a kid I recognize from the basketball court, a lefty who shoots threes and yells at everybody else to play defense—are rolling joints on the kitchen table and putting them into plastic bags. They've moved the TV onto the kitchen counter. In the movie, guys dressed in black carry out acts of vandalism on an unsuspecting city.

"What's that smell?"

"We're making soap," Charles says. "You render the fat by boiling away the tallow." He holds up a copy of the *Fight Club* book. "It's all right here. Right in the goddam book." He's giving me the serious look, the one that reminds me of his father. "Soap. Napalm. Pipe bombs. Everything! This book is like, literally, a recipe for disaster, man."

My pasta pot is filled with pasty goop, a thick liquid bubbling in sickly gasps. Lumpy is stirring, dressed in hundred dollar shoes and black Tommy Hilfiger jeans. He skims white stuff off the top, drops it into our Tupperware.

I can't breathe. "My pasta pot," is all I can say.

"What?"

"My pasta pot."

Charles grabs me by the arm and steers me toward the bedroom.

He shuts the door. "Look, I know we're going a little crazy here." He waves his hands around in a flutter. "But there's something there, man. There's something in that movie, in this book. I swear to god."

"This doesn't help me, you know," I say. "I have work to do, bills, the court thing is coming up."

"And the neat thing." This is how he's always referred to the things I have to do. The neat thing.

"But this is more real than that shit," he says. "Think about my old job. Trying to get people to put money in the funds that made *me* the most money—what the fuck was that? Our fathers are our vision of God, right?" He waves the book at me. "That's how my fucking father made all his money. Is that real? Were those couches real? The entertainment center? Come on, Joe. We *are* the middle children of history. You think the Pottery Barn is gonna save us?"

"It's just, it's not helping. That's a movie. You're not Brad Pitt, Charles."

"Chuck. My name is Chuck." He stares at me. I can tell he's trying to morph his face into Pitt's by sheer will, pushing his lips out, willing his cheekbones higher. But with his pinched eyes and pouty face, he's always going to look like the rich brat that he is. Put him in a $2,000 suit and he's already the spitting image of Charles Senior.

"Come on," is all I can say.

107

"What?"

"You know."

"I don't, man."

"I was there in college when you went through the rastafarian thing," I say. "Sorry, *rasta-far-eye*. The whiteboy dreadlocks. Then the Grateful Dead, with the tie-dyes and all the tapes with things like Meadowlands 5-8-86 written on top. And then the *Swingers* phase, the chain wallet and the Fonzie wardrobe. You kept saying 'It's so money' and 'Let's go find some beautiful babies'."

He pulls himself erect against the door, folds his arms, pushes his biceps out with the front of his hands. "This is different."

"You guys are making soap and rolling joints in the kitchen. In my pasta pot. The table is gone. The couches, the entertainment center…"

"That's what I mean. This isn't just fashion."

"I can't live like this. This is really bad for me."

"Project Mayhem!" someone shouts from the living room.

"Look," Charles says, "what if something happened? What if you could join us?"

"I can't sit down before I do the thing with the lights. The magazines. I can't…"

"I know. But maybe someday." Charles smiles and closes the door on his way out.

I look at the bottle. One two three four…twenty-nine Percocets. I take two and edit the beta blockers monograph until my eyelids burn. I turn the sleep machine up as loud as it will go and stare at the ceiling.

• • •

A week goes by. I live like a shadow, like a housepet, confined to my space. It's like sharing a haunted house with a fraternity of ghosts: I know they're there, I hear them in my sleep, I clean up their mess in the morning, or when I come home from work. Every now and then I catch a glimpse, retreating through the door as I'm going into the bathroom, or sleeping off whatever it is they do, Lumpy and Lefty crashing in the basement like military recruits. Little mounds of pot stems appear on the carpet like crop circles.

I slip in and out of the bathroom like a cat. If I could set up a litterbox in my bedroom, I would.

I can't tell what they're doing. Going out at night and coming home late in the morning. Copies of *Fight Club* are scattered around the house like hymnals in a church. I watch the newspaper for signs of civil disobedience. I stare at every waiter, busboy, or garage attendant. None of them seems to bear the casually battered faces, the broken noses, split lips, and black eyes of their cinematic brethren.

One day I wake up and find the entire living room spray-painted red. Across the back wall, in black, it says "Project Mayhem." The paint mixes with the lingering stink of soap and it smells dangerous, like the whole place could blow at any minute. The living room blinds are open. Neighbor Betsy pushes her stroller. She catches my eye, turns away, and hustles up the street.

I walk into the kitchen to start my coffee. My keys are on the floor. My wallet is sitting on the counter. There's a big red thumbprint on the black leather.

A knock at the door. It's the Russians. They're both smoking cigarettes and sucking from Big Gulp cups, still wearing the Jiffy Lube coveralls.

fight club club

"There's nothing out there," I say.

"We come inside now," the bigger one says. He elbows past me. "He say to come in, join Project Mayhem."

"You can't have any of the stuff." I try not to look toward my bedroom door.

"Eventully," he says, "these thing you have. They start to have you. We do not want more thing from you."

• • •

As the court date gets closer, I throw myself into work. I spend twelve hours a day behind my desk. I skip lunches. I'm losing weight, growing black marks under my eyes. I lose myself in it, the simple typos, split infinitives and hanging participles, the music of punctuation. The *Chicago Manual of Style* is my Bible. It's all right there, right in the book—the rules for everything. No moral dilemmas, no figuring it out as you go along, no second-guessing or Charles looking over your shoulder. Just rules, plain and simple. Black and white. Right and wrong.

• • •

It's payday, end of the month, and I'm double checking the clonazepam monograph when Mr. Bannister knocks on my door. He's holding the methylphenidate monograph and his face is bright red, his mouth a grim scab. "We have to talk," he says. He sits in my guest chair. One of its legs is broken and he sinks down, almost topples. He stands and motions me into the bad chair. We switch positions.

"You know I had a lot of trust in you," he says.

110

I nod. Had? I can feel a tingle in the back of my head. I put my hand over the *Chicago Manual of Style*.

"You've been a model employee," he says. "That's why I want to give you this chance, before…" He looks at the monograph and shakes his head. "Did anybody see this before you sent it to copy?"

"I'm an associate. I have copy approval."

"Goddamit, Joseph, what were you thinking? Is this some kind of political statement?" He throws the monograph in my direction and it falls to the ground. I lean to pick it up and the chair goes down with a crash. The arm pushes into my abdomen like I've been punched. The air goes out of me and my head hits the floor with a *thwock*. I let it go for a second, enjoying the black, allowing myself to slip. It would be nice to let go, to sleep.

Bannister helps me up. I stare at him until he points again to the monograph. APIC leaflets all begin with the conditions for which the pharmaceutical is prescribed:

> "Methylphenidate, or Ritalin, is prescribed
> to prevent boat-rocking by antsy children and
> disaffected teenagers. But hey kids, listen up.
> Ritalin can be injected (this is referred to as "west
> coasting") to obtain a powerful high similar to
> that of heroin, or can also used in combination
> with heroin (this is called a "speedball"), or—hey,
> why not!—with both cocaine and heroin, for a
> more potent effect."

I can't believe I'm reading this. What's going on? I feel like I'm going to throw up. I'm sweating. Bannister holds up the release-to-print form and there's my signature. But this isn't what I approved.

Then it hits me. Charles. One week ago. The keys on the floor, the thumbprint on my wallet. And there it is, slipped into the Potential Side Effects listing: "feelings of lightheadedness, black or tarry stools, project mayhem, drymouth…"

"I'm sorry," Bannister says. "I don't really have a choice. You have to go."

This is where Ed Norton would beat himself up, knock his own face into a bloody pulp and come away with some kind of movie-only severance package. I shake Bannister's hand, lead him out the door. I take my clock radio and mug-warmer, the two pictures that I keep in my desk drawer—Mom and Dad looking stoned and aimless, Charles and me at graduation. I put it all into my bag and walk slowly to the elevator. I take out the bottle and count them, then dry-swallow five Percocets and put the rest, loose, in my pocket.

• • •

When I get home, my bed and desk are sitting out on the curb. The Geo Metro is parked in my spot. One two three four five six seven steps to the door. Charles and James are sitting on their lawn chairs, dressed in rumpled tuxedoes. They're watching the movie and leafing through *FHM* and *Maxim*.

"What the hell do you think you're doing?" I say. I turn the lights on off on.

Charles looks at the sad little box of office stuff in my hand. "We spend our days working jobs we hate to buy shit that we don't need," he says. James just gives me the thumbs down. I lock the door.

There's an explosion on the TV and we all look over to see Ed Norton sticking a gun into his own mouth.

Somebody has spray painted "Project Mayhem" on the carpet. Pizza boxes and 7-11 hot dog containers cover the floor. The whole place smells like a combination of locker room and bar— sweat and soap, smoke and stale beer.

"I loved that job," I say. "Everything about it."

"Today will be the best day of your life. Things will taste better, you'll feel better..." I pick up the magazines and start to put them in order. Charles knocks them out of my hand. "What are you doing?" he asks.

"What do you think, you cured me?" I grab at the magazines.

"I've been trying to help you for the past ten years," Charles says. He's looking out the window, watching Neighbor Bill and son Benjamin tippling down the street on brand new bicycles. "You believe that shit, James," he asks. "I've been trying to help this little OCD pussy for ten years and this is what I get."

I jiggle the Percocets, loose in my pocket. I swallow two, suck them down like Altoids.

"What am I supposed to do now, Charles? I had my life made here. I had it figured out, a system. I loved that job." I pull the *Chicago Manual of Style* out of my box. The weight feels good in my hands. "What am I supposed to do?"

Charles smiles. He holds it like a preacher or a salesman—no shame and no mercy. "Join us," he says. "Join Project Mayhem."

"Oh god."

"I'm serious. This is real, Joe. Like I told you. Not fashion anymore."

"Charles."

"Join Project Mayhem."

For a second, I'm filled with love for Charles. It would feel good to stop fighting everything. It would be as easy as sleeping— just let go, follow orders, allow somebody else to make all the decisions.

"I can't."

"You can."

"I can't walk up to the front door without counting my steps, Charles. I can't sit down before I arrange the magazines, check the locks and the oven—"

"Know what we did today?" There's a gleam in his eye that I haven't seen since he almost got kicked out of college for the second time. "James and me got jobs as waiters."

I open the *Style Manual*. A sentence catches my eye: *When a number begins a sentence, it is always spelled out.*

"So we get jobs as waiters for this fancy catering company downtown. We're in the elevator, coming up from the kitchen, and we piss right in the seafood bisque." He high-fives James. "Next week, we're gonna lace the chicken noodle with shrooms."

"Shroom fucking noodle soup, dude," James says.

The *Manual* says, *A comma follows names or words used in direct address and informal correspondence.*

"And that's not all." He grabs my arm and for a second it's almost like we're kids again, like he's explaining Dungeons and Dragons or what it's like to kiss a girl. "Dude, we've been doing some serious social commentary at night, following right along with the movie, with the book even, planting these messages around town and shit. That thing in the paper about the graffiti on the metro? That was us, man."

Years are expressed in numerals unless they stand at the beginning of a sentence.

"Are you even listening," Charles asks. "Have you heard anything? Do you notice anything that happens around here?"

"I can't join," is all I can say.

Charles pushes his head down to his knees. The lawn chair strains under his weight. He pulls his hair and makes a growling sound. Finally he stands up. He's trying to morph his face into Brad Pitt's. James is watching us like we're a big screen TV.

"Hit me," Charles says. "Hit me as hard as you can." He sticks his pudgy face up into mine. He pushes me, hard, in the chest. "Hit me, you OCD pussy!"

"My court date is next week." I picture the Russians picking me off the curb, loading me into their Geo. Everything is starting to get fuzzy, lights popping soft and bright in the corners of my eyes.

"Come on!" he yells. "Feel something. Hit me!"

"This isn't a fucking movie," I say. I'm clutching the *Style Guide*.

He pushes me again in the chest. He takes the magazines and scatters them over the floor. He empties out my work box.

I watch my things fall onto the dirty carpet. Should I pick up the magazines first, or my pictures? The pens and pencils or the pieces of the clock radio? What would it be like to really join them? Could I do it?

Charles lunges for the *Style Guide* and I pull back. "That's what you need," he says. "A little less guide, a little more mayhem. You need this, Joe." He takes a step toward me.

I lead with the spine of the book, chop hard into his cheek. He yelps like a puppy and goes down. "What the fuck, Joe?" he screams. A streak of blood worms onto the rented tuxedo.

I grab the *Style Manual* again and open to a random page:

115

fight club club

Particular centuries are spelled out and lowercased. I break the spine
on his back. The pages spill out onto the floor. I use my fists. First
my right until it hurts. Then my left. It hurts. It feels good.

The Movie Soundtrack to Our Lives

The Movie Soundtrack to Our Lives will be warm, funny, raucous, and soulful. Mostly, however, like the relationship that spawned the movie that required the soundtrack, it will be bittersweet. The Movie Soundtrack to Our Lives will feature new artists (Beth Orton, Morcheeba), old favorites (Bob Dylan, Cannonball Adderley), and more than a few surprises (like I'm going to list those out here, in the first paragraph). It will be like a mixtape from a really cool friend. It will not, in fact, be unlike the mixtapes I once made for you.

Which I would like back.

The Movie Soundtrack to Our Lives will probably open with "Tear Stained Eye" by Son Volt. The first scene of the movie will be a riff on the "Stayin' Alive" opening in *Saturday Night Fever*, which I don't think you've ever even seen because you haven't seen any of the Essential movies, like *Cool Hand Luke* or *Office Space*. And don't misinterpret that, in the way you know you do, either, into me saying that *Saturday Night Fever* is somehow Essential because it's not Essential in the way *True Romance* or *Harold and Maude* might be considered Essential. It is, however, Seminal, in that it's a movie almost everybody has seen and from which we take a lot of our modern movie touchpoints. I can see you now, sitting in Jimmy's Brother's basement, you and Jimmy's Brother laughing about me considering *Saturday Night Fever* Essential when it is really Seminal and the difference is totally lost on the both of you.

So the opening is a steadycam shot, focused on my black Chuck Taylors, moving slow down the broken sidewalks of our shitty hometown. It will pan across to Jimmy's workboots, moving alongside, with his trademark little limp. And then your Docs come into the frame. Slow pan up your long legs, the Army surplus cutoffs, CBGB t-shirt that I later learned you bought at Target (but, like me, for the opening sequence, at least, the audience will be fooled), and then the face with your little sunburned, upturned nose, your blue eyes with that look like they're telling a joke that I guess I know now I'll never, ever get, and the brown hair with the little streaks of blonde. All the while, Jay Farrar singing with that sugary rough alt country voice, "I would meet you anywhere the western sun meets the air..."

The Movie Soundtrack to Our Lives is going to be one motherfucker of a tearjerker.

From the intro, there will be a slow build-up. A progression of mellow to sunny to boisterous songs that will follow the movie version of me and you through the courtship phase, which I guess you'd also call the Month of July, seeing as how it's now August and Jimmy's Fucking Brother is probably nuzzling himself up to you right now, tracing your freckles with his hairy fingers, manhandling your buttonflys.

Some songs I'm thinking about for this part of the movie: "Concrete Sky" by Beth Orton, "Lotta Love" by Neil Young, Morcheeba's "Sao Paulo," and maybe a little something from My Morning Jacket or some old Elvis Costello.

Now that I think about it, this part will probably only be like two songs, since we only had maybe four real dates and you spent most of one throwing up into the bed of my truck while I held your silky hair and watched the cars come in and out of the high school parking lot. And there was the one where we went to the movies and right after you said you had cramps and had to get home, with that look on your face like Women Problems and me with no counter to that move.

Still, there'll be that one scene where it all comes together, where we're driving around and the moon is bouncing off the alfalfa and you're smiling and calm and not drunk or even smoking anything. That will be a nice part of the movie, the part that people remember, that makes them think about their own lives and loves, maybe reach across the theater seat with that I Love You look I see other people making at each other. For that part it'll be something slow and rolling, maybe "It Makes No Difference" by The Band, if the irony of that wouldn't be too heavy-handed. But you never did notice irony very much anyway, or else I don't think you'd be with Jimmy's Brother right now and I wouldn't have to even be creating the Movie Soundtrack of Our Lives.

I'm going to be watching eBay, and if you and Jimmy's Brother try to sell those mixtapes, I'm going to be all over it.

The party scene out at Jimmy's parent's cabin will be the big shift in the movie, from the courtship/Month of July lead-in to the big First Time and what I know now to be the Beginning of the End. The Jimmy's Parents Cabin Scene will be kind of like that "Louie Louie" scene from *Animal House*, all of us singing along, arms around each other, sopping drunk and loving life. Jimmy's Brother will be like a shadowy presence in that scene, like

Neidermyer sneaking around the background while you and me and Jimmy sing at the table like grown-ups and brothers in arms.

We'll probably use Dylan's "Quinn the Eskimo" for that scene, even though I know and I know you know it was really "Sister Christian" by Night Ranger.

You'd probably like "Sister Christian" better than "Quinn the Eskimo," anyway.

Sometimes I don't know what I saw in you in the first place.

For that night, the First Time scene of Mellow Lovemaking on Jimmy Parent's Cabin's Porch, I'm thinking we stick with Dylan and use "Tonight I'm Staying Here with You." I know what you're thinking—too much Dylan, too fast a song for the scene. But as usual I'm thinking like three steps ahead of you, like Pele, but with music, and we'll probably get Ryan Adams to Wonderwall it, same lyrics, but with a shitload of echo, just his own guitar and maybe a little organ in the background, slowed down and mournful. Are you understanding the irony that version will impart to the scene?

But like I said, you and irony never really connected, did you?

I'll probably include something from that band Soundtrack of Our Lives, just because a band called Soundtrack of Our Lives in the Movie Soundtrack to Our Lives is just a total postmodern mind-fuck and I think it might make your little head explode just to see that in the song listing because you never did let me finish explaining what postmodern meant anyway, that night we watched *Pulp Fiction* and I wanted to concentrate on the dialogue and all you wanted to do was suck down as much peach Schnapps as you possibly could.

For the record, just so you know, peach Schnapps is not cool. I can tell you that now. If you go off to college and start telling people you drink peach Schnapps, the jig is going to be up real fast.

But all of this is really leading up to the climax. The part where you break up with me, where you get all distant and stop returning calls and I can practically smell Jimmy's Brother's fucking scent on you, is going to be the real centerpiece of the movie.

"Telling detail," is what the critics will say. "A painfully accurate portrait of fading love."

"What a freakin' bitch."

You thought that *Garden State* soundtrack was all mellow and sadsack? Sit back and listen. That *Scrubs* goofball has nothing on me. I'm talking about something from *Kind of Blue*. Some Chet Baker. Iron and Wine, who are like a new, hip version of that Nick Drake from the Volkswagon commercial. "Mercy, Mercy, Mercy" by Cannonball Adderley. Who is Cannonball Adderley, you might ask? Remember when that song came on the truck stereo and I said "That's the song I want them to play at my funeral" and you kind of laughed until you realized I was serious and so was Cannonball Adderley and then we listened to it like ten times in a row outside the mall until you said you had to pee and I kind of suspected all along that you were just faking to ruin the moment and because Jimmy's Brother worked at Sbarros? Remember that?

You wouldn't.

And maybe that's the whole point of the Movie Soundtrack to Our Lives—to set the record straight, not just for me but for you, for Jimmy's Brother, everybody. Maybe the point is that even though a little shit like Jimmy's Brother can tear us apart, music can still bring people together. The right people. The right music. Together.

So listen up. Think about it. You might learn something. Maybe we all will.

They make those sequels all the time.

Thorn

"Now for the moment you'ns have been waiting for," I say into the microphone, trying to get some jump into my voice, despite everything. "Let's give it on up for…Tawny and Brad!" I'm supposed to say "Mr. and Mrs. Brad Reichenbach" but I can't do it, not for seventy-five bucks an hour, not for a million. Tawny's mom shoots me a look and I know my tip is shot. I pretend I don't see her, cue up Night Ranger's "Sister Christian" for the first dance, and try to ignore the fact that the only woman I'll ever love is now Mrs. Brad Reichenbach.

Tawny is in a group hug with her mother and her fat Aunt Francie. They turn down the lights in the firehall and she pulls Brad onto the dance floor. Her blond hair, white dress, and tan skin shine against the red Budweiser sign and I swear to god she's actually glowing, like a supermodel or a UFO. She waves to her sister and cousin. Brad pushes his head into Tawny's neck. He looks dull and stupid next to her, like one of those Siamese twins that come out all shriveled up and the other one has to get it cut out or lug it around like a birth defect for the rest of their life.

I steady myself on the console, accidentally nudge the treble a few decibels, and feedback squawks through the speakers. I pretend to be tuning the mix. When I look up, everybody turns away except Francie. She caught us once at the end of a date, steaming up my Falcon, me with one hand halfway down the back of Tawny's jeans and the other working up her shirt. This is six years ago, when Tawny was 17 and I was 22, but Francie's had it out for me ever since.

Night Ranger is grooving into the chorus—*you're motorin'… what's your price for flight*—when Tawny's mother jerks her thumb toward the dance floor and sets her jaw. "Ladies and gentlemen," I say, "Tawny and Brad invite you to join them in their…*first dance.*"

"Sister Christian" fades and I put on "Every Rose Has Its Thorn" by Poison. Tawny's mom gives me another look.

I follow "Every Rose" with "Love Hurts" by Nazareth. People drift back to their tables. Aunt Francie scowls in my direction. Tawny's mother sneaks up behind and pinches me on the back of the arm. "Cut the shit mister," she says. I punch up Cinderella's "Don't Know What You Got ('Til It's Gone)," finish the rest of my beer, and pull another one out of the cooler.

Tawny and Brad get up to cut the cake. This is where I'm supposed to start my big DJ routine. I have a whole act, get the crowd all riled up. You get married in Kratzer County, I'm pretty much the guy you want for the reception. I look at Tawny, her sleepy eyes and perfect nose, the blond hair feathered back just so. She's already taken off her shoes and there's a patch of something—Long Island iced tea would be my guess—stained into the middle of her dress.

Brad looks clean and harmless, like one of those guys from the asshole fraternity in *Animal House*.

I hit the back button and "Don't Know What You Got" starts up again. I twist the volume. Tawny stomps over, her tan face turning orange and bruised-looking. I watch her breasts do the bouncy thing as she gets closer.

"This is my special goddam day," she says, "and you ain't gonna ruin it. You had your chance but you fucked Rita. So do your thing or we'll rip up that check and play your stupid mix tapes."

Her jaw twitches a little and I can see where she packed make-up over her zits. So she still has the mix tapes. Cinderella winds up and there's a space where it's all silent. Brad coughs. I punch up Billy Idol's "Mony Mony."

"The things we do for love," I say. "Okay!" I shout into the microphone. "Are we ready to get this party started?" Billy Idol starts in with *HEY… mony mony…*

After five minutes, I have them dancing. After ten minutes, they're sweating. Men take off their jackets, women kick their heels under tables. After a half hour, they're all mine. I give them AC/DC, Hank Junior, some old disco. I run through all the favorites. During "Y.M.C.A." I make everybody start in with the hand motions, even Tawny's grandmother out there on her walker, making Y's and M's with one arm. I feel like Dale Earnhardt behind the wheel, Eddie Van Halen wailing away in front of a hundred thousand.

Brad dances all stiff-limbed, like a Ken doll brought to life. He keeps slipping away to check his cell phone. Tawny is all over the place, pulling folks onto the dance floor one minute, doing shots with the girls from the supermarket the next. When I play "Margaritaville," she leads a conga line right out in the middle of Market Street. By the time I punch up "Wonderful Tonight" and head out for some air, her dress has a ring of gray stains along the bottom and she's got a bandage leaking blood over her right big toe. We catch eyes. "Thanks," she says. "Asshole."

I make a vow then and there to do anything I can to get her back.

thorn

• • •

I make reservations at Lover's Haven on Sunday. On Monday,
I work my eight hour shift, then max out my Visa on a cash
advance. On Tuesday, I do the same with the Discover.

Near the end of my Wednesday shift I pretend to bump
into the new waitress. "Watch where you're going, sugar," I
say. She nods and works her way around me. "So," I say, "I was
wondering…"

"I have a boyfriend," she says. "Fryer-boy creep."

Dennis, the assistant manager, pulls me into the walk-in. "You
want a lawsuit, Wayne? Can't do that shit no more."

"I was just asking."

"Yeah, well, don't."

"What about you? Few beers after work?"

He waddles out of the walk-in and I follow. He waves at the
order slips stacked up over my station. "Lotsa people waiting for
wings and fries out there."

That night, I call Lover's Haven and ask for Tawny's room.
"I'm sorry," the woman says, "they've got the 'do not disturb' on
the phone."

I hang up, go into the yard, and smash a half-case of
Budweiser against the side of the garage.

I sit down on the stoop and watch the dark glass glitter in
the moonlight. The neighbors are having a couple of beers on the
porch. They've got Willie Nelson going and "Blue Eyes Crying"
echoes tinny across the yard. My stomach is starting to cramp. I
haven't felt right since the wedding.

I take the portable speakers out of the car, wire them up to the
CD on the patio, and turn *Zeppelin One* up to five. Robert Plant

wails away: *Good times bad times you know I've had my shaaaay-yur...*

The neighbors turn up their music and Willie Nelson starts up with "Crazy." I can barely hear the melody of "Babe I'm Gonna Leave You." I turn the boombox to seven.

"Come on, Wayne!" the neighbor shouts. "We're having a fucking moment over here, man."

Beer stink rises up from the broken bottles. A car pulls into my driveway and I stand up. It pulls out, turns around, and burns rubber in the other direction. I twist the volume to ten and go into the kitchen for more beer.

• • •

I'm off Thursday, so I sleep late then head to the strip bar on route 45. Two girls are dancing, five guys sitting around the bar. One of the girls is blond and skinny, with floppy breasts and long legs. She smiles while she dances, makes small talk with the tables.

I order two beers and two shots of whiskey. "How much for a lap dance?" I ask the blond.

She hops off the bar and sits in my lap. She smells like sweat and sweet-tarts. "I like you," she says. "Fifty bucks."

"How about ten?"

She grabs my hand and walks toward the back of the bar, where a sheet is stretched across the hallway. She leads me onto a dirty couch. I hand her a ten and she straddles me. "I'm Florida," she says, "what's your name?"

"What kinda name is that?"

"I'm new here," she says. "And these other two girls? They were already Dakota and Carolina, so I'm Florida. Plus I wanna

127

move there, where it's sunny." She holds her arms up over her head and starts gyrating, pushes her breasts up into my chin.

"Wait a minute," I say. "I got a question for you."

"You can't touch me," she says, loud, in the direction of the curtain. Then she leans over and whispers, "fifty for a BJ."

"That's not what I'm talking about," I say, although in my mind I'm doing the math, trying to figure if I could subtract fifty and still have enough for a three days in the Poconos. "How'd you like to go on a little vacation?"

● ● ●

It's a three hour drive to Lover's Haven, and I go through the first four Van Halen albums while Florida paints her nails. She gives me a quiz from *Cosmopolitan*. I score in the Red Hot Lover range and she gets this little smile on her face and asks do I want my toenails painted. She's twenty-one and lived in Kratzer County all her life. She's been stripping six months, hoping to save enough money for plane fare, or a car that'll get her into the sun for good.

My stomach churns and we have to stop four times so I can use the bathroom, once to buy another bottle of Pepto Bismol. I haven't been right since I maxed out those cards. The wad is stuffed into my pocket, a roll of twenties about the size of a handgrenade. I haven't slept in three days, thinking about how I screwed it all up, about that stupid thing with Rita, and those nights with Tawny in the Falcon, her perfumey smell and the way she'd smile and close her eyes, sing along in that raspy voice when I'd play the right song.

"We're here!" Florida yells, when she sees the Lover's Haven billboard. She punches me in the arm. We follow a two-lane road through tall pines, past a little lake, and into the parking lot. We wander through big, heart-shaped doors into a wide room filled with life-size sculptures of Romans standing around naked. In one corner, a fountain dribbles white noise; a fireplace burns in the other.

We check in and a woman with bright blond hair and a face the color of fried chicken pops out from behind a doorway. "I'm Bonnie!" she says. "Your entertainment manager!" Her handshake is strong. She's short, with a gleam in her eye like a cheerleader gone berserk. She hands me a folder and a key with a heart-shaped tag that says "Key to Paradise." She opens the folder. "Now that's your activities list for the day," she says. "Volleyball, fishing, shuffleboard. Also your menus for the day, and your group assignment."

"Group?"

"Your dinner group! You eat with the same folks every night. It's really super! You'll make lifelong friends!"

"Oh, we have a couple of friends here, thought maybe we'd look them up," I say. "Tawny and Brad...uh, Reichenbach."

"Super!" Bonnie shouts. "What a cute couple! Honeymooners! We'll put them in your group. You all can catch up! And don't forget tomorrow's the DJ Disco Dance! DJ Disco Lance from Philadelphia."

"I do a little bit of that myself," I say. "DJ, that is."

"Then you won't want to miss it," Bonnie says. "DJ Disco Lance is the best. We're known for it. Now head right on up to that room and have a super time!"

Our room is as big as my house. The bed is round, with red sheets. "Oh my God," Florida says, "I feel like I'm on MTV Cribs." There's a little bucket labeled "Love Supply: In Case of

Emergency, Unwrap." Florida rips it open. There's a package of Lover's Lotion, a jug of bubble bath, a big red feather, and two little bottles of champagne. She paws through the stuff and I feel a little action in my pants. I will it down, thinking about Tawny and Brad opening that same package. A heart-shaped hot-tub is bubbling in one corner. Florida strips down and hops in. "Come on, baby," she says.

"That ain't why we're here," I say, although I am tempted. She pouts and pushes her breasts out a little. I go into the bedroom, pick up the phone, and dial information. "Philadelphia," I say, "a business called DJ Disco Lance."

• • •

The dining room is like something from *Titanic*, all stairs, railings, red carpet, and white tablecloths. A guy in a tuxedo leads us to the table. Brad is talking with an old guy with a beard and a three-piece suit while Tawny whispers into the waitress' ear.

"Hey guys," I say. "Ain't this a surprise."

Tawny smiles at first, then I see her wheels turning and her face scrunches up. Florida waves. Tawny grabs my arm. "No!" she says.

I smile like we're joking around. "What're you doing here?" I say.

"Duh," Tawny says.

"I thought you were going to Ocean City. Me and Florida just wanted a little getaway, thought this place looked cool." I introduce myself to the bearded guy and his scared-looking wife. "Paul Jackowitz," he says, "and that's the wife, Brandy."

"Well isn't this a coincidence?" Brad says. I give him my innocent face. He stands up and I follow him to the bar. He orders two bourbons and flashes his room key. "I know what you're up to," he says. "And if you think for a minute I'm going to let you get away with this, you're stupider than I thought." He drinks the bourbon in one motion. "So why don't you just take your little hooker friend home and get out of our life?"

I take a sip. "First off, she's a stripper not a hooker. Second, why the hell would I wanna go on vacation with my ex-girlfriend and her new husband?" I finish the bourbon. "I ain't that stupid, Brad."

He stands all stiff and I can see he's struggling not to hit me. The bartender walks over. "Trouble fellas?"

Brad shakes his head and walks back to the table. I knock back two more bourbons and a beer on his tab. When I get back, Brad and Tawny's spots are empty. Florida is whispering into the bearded guy's ear while his wife pushes prime rib around her plate.

I try to enjoy my meal but I keep looking at Tawny's empty seat, the pink lipstick ring along the top of her glass. I wonder what she was wearing under her dress.

Bonnie bounces over to our table, kneels down, and puts her hand on my shoulder. "I have to ask you for a huge favor," she says. "We have a problem. With the DJ? DJ Lance? From Philadelphia?" I nod. "Something happened. Some kind of, like, death threat. He can't make it."

"Too bad," I say.

"It's really…not super. And normally I would never do this, but we're in a real pinch, and I think you did say you were a DJ? A professional?" I nod. She scrunches her hands up like a prayer. "Is there any way you could help us out tomorrow night?"

I pretend to be surprised. "What do you think, honey?" I look to Florida. She's giggling with the bearded guy.

131

thorn

I turn to Bonnie. "I think I could help you out."

• • •

In the morning, Bonnie has the bellboys carry my equipment up from the van, speakers and board into the dining room and CDs up to my room. I lay all her favorites out on the bed, Tawny's Top 50.

My stomach rumbles and I pound on the bathroom door. Florida has been in there for an hour. My insides are turning like a can full of nightcrawlers. I haven't really slept in days. "I have to go!" I shout.

"Like I give a care," she says, but she opens the door. Her face is red and wet and she looks young without makeup. She pushes past me and hits the jets on the hot tub. I dive into the bathroom and land on the bowl with little time to spare. MTV starts blaring from the other room. I relieve myself and have one moment where I forget about everything. It's clean and warm in the bathroom and the towels are thick, white, and fluffy. For a minute everything seems perfect, like it should be in a place like this.

But then I remember everything I have to do. I chug some Pepto and get back to my equipment. I have to be mobile, can't be stuck behind the board all night. Eventually, I'll need to get her alone.

I take apart the portable speakers, wire them together with my discman, and then duct tape the whole thing into my jean jacket. I poke some holes into the front so the speakers can play through. It barely fits around my shoulders and the wires jab me in the belly, but when I hit play, sure enough, there's Night Ranger sounding tinny but loud, pecking out the opening piano of "Sister

132

Christian." I turn it up and feel the bass rumbling in my gut.

"What the hell you doing?" Florida asks.

I put the jean jacket down. "Don't worry about it."

"I don't get it." She says. "All this for that girl? She don't even want you."

"She deserves better than that asshole."

"I don't know, he seems like he treats her pretty nice. He's nice looking. And you said he's rich." The hot tub boils in the corner. In the windows, I can see the mountains, cool and green, the little lake shiny with the morning sun. "Plus which," she says, "didn't you say you cheated on her? That guy ain't the cheating type."

"He's an asshole!" I poke my finger into her chest, too hard, and she jumps back, slips, falls hard on her butt. She rolls over, rubbing her hip and crying softly. "Dang," she whispers. "Dang dang dang." The jump goes out of my chest and I can feel the blood moving into my face. I want to say I'm sorry, but then she sits up and something's changed in her eyes, hardness settling in like ice over a puddle.

"Me and Tawny, we belong together," I say.

Florida gets up shaky and wobbles into the hot tub. She turns MTV as loud as it will go and cracks the mini-champagne bottle from the Love Supply kit. She holds the bubble bath up to the light, then empties it into the tub. I point at the sign that says "Please no bubble bath in hot tub." She gives me the finger and opens the other bottle of champagne.

• • •

When Florida goes for her pedicure, I take a walk by Tawny's room. The hall is empty, room service trays scattered like candy wrappers. There's nobody around and I realize I'm hungry. A half-burger and an uneaten chicken sandwich are sitting outside Brad and Tawny's room. Thirty dollars worth of lunch and they just leave it there. I lean toward the door and listen. I hear giggles and the hum of the hot tub. I pound three times on the door and everything stops but the tub. My heart cranks a Bo Diddly beat – *boom-boom, boom, boom-boom, boom.*

Tawny opens the door. "That was quick..." she starts. Then she mutters "shit" and steps out into the hall. "We thought you were the champagne guy." She's in a towel. The bottom of her hair is wet, but the top is still feathered back just so. I try not to think about Brad waiting in the tub, concentrate on Tawny and the smooth tops of her thighs, the tanline peeking under her towel.

I'm all stuck. I feel like running away, like taking her in my arms, like clocking her one right in her perfect little nose. "I love you" comes out before I can hold it back.

She shakes her head. "You don't love me, Wayne." I take a step and she puts a hand up. Her palm is wet and hot on my chest. "So just leave us alone. You gotta leave us alone."

"I don't know."

She stares until my eyes turn toward the carpet. "Maybe you wanna think about it this way, then," she says. "You can't compete with Brad. Nowhere close. We're rich, Wayne. This kinda place, I don't know what you had to do to be here, but this is the kinda place we'll be staying in forever. You gotta have money to make it, Wayne. You ain't got it. Brad does."

I look down at the room service trays. "I said I love you."

The elevator dings and a kid in a red uniform pushes a cart down the hall. "That would be our champagne and strawberries," she says.

I'm about a quarter of the way into the bourbon when Florida comes back. Her face is flushed and she's wearing a new leather jacket and matching pants. She throws her purse on top of my CDs. "Hey!" I grab her arm. "That was the second set."

"Mr. Jackowitz!" she yells.

The bearded guy from dinner comes into the room. He's wearing a turtleneck and tweed jacket, with corduroy pants and bright white tennis shoes. He's making a constipated face, his fists clenched, chest puffed out like a body builder. "She's not gonna put up with your shit anymore, fella," he says. Florida puts her arm around him and nods.

"What shit?" I say. "We don't even know each other."

"What I hear, that hasn't stopped you none."

"We're going down south," Florida says. "South Carolina."

She kisses him on the cheek and he blushes and whispers, "North Carolina, honeypie." I can see that he's serious, but having doubts, like a guy waiting for the car salesman to get back from talking it over with his manager.

"What about Mrs. Jackowitz?"

He shakes his head and squeezes Florida's shoulder. She wriggles free and starts throwing stuff into her suitcase. "I don't know why I ever agreed to do this," she says, "with such a loser. Still hung up on his high school girlfriend or whatever. I don't even think you're very good at that playing the music stuff you're so serious about," she waves at my CDs, "you just play the same crap as everybody else."

"That ain't the point," I say, and start picking CDs off the floor.

"Whatever." She stuffs Lover's Haven towels into her suitcase, fills the seams with little bottles of conditioner and hand cream. Jackowitz steps onto the bulging suitcase and she wrestles it closed.

"Don't follow us, buddy," he says. "And do me a favor—don't tell Brandy where we're headed." He blushes again and huffs out with Florida's suitcase.

• • •

"Check one two rock roll," I say into the microphone. I'm finishing my setup, taping down cables and cueing up the first set. The jean jacket boombox is sitting in a corner and I'm sipping at a mixture of bourbon and Pepto. It tastes like a mint julep made of cardboard. Bonnie bounces over and squeezes my shoulder. "Look at all that equipment," she says. "So many cables and, oh my goodness!" She jumps back, covers her mouth, and points to the little pistol-shaped lighter tucked behind the mixing board.

"Sorry," I say. "Some of the places I play, that's a necessary piece of equipment." I hold it toward the wall and click the trigger so flame pops out. I fake like I'm lighting a cigarette and Bonnie laughs. I make a big show of putting it into my gym bag, zipping up like I'm locking a safe.

She looks at the crowd, starting to fill in. "Any time you're ready."

I check the table but there's no sign of Tawny and Brad. Mrs. Jackowitz sits by herself, looking small and frail, her white dress melting into the tablecloth.

Bonnie gives me the thumbs up. I lean into the microphone. "Lovebirds!" I yell, trying to force my voice up toward the second floor. "Are you ready to party?"

• • •

There's no sign of her through the first set. I'm working on my third bourbon when I see the flash of blond hair off to the side. Tawny and Brad make their way over to the table. Tawny squeezes Mrs. Jackowitz's shoulder and Brad kisses her hand.

I get through half the bottle and the bottom twenty of Tawny's Top Fifty. She doesn't even seem to notice, just eats her meal, quiet, every now and then leaning over to whisper something in Brad's ear. She looks small and sad. Brad gives me his best Clint Eastwood.

When they stand to leave, I pull the pistol lighter out of the bag and stuff it into my pocket. Walking feels funny. Everything is foggy and too-quick. Tawny says something to Brad and they move into the hall.

I pull out the lighter. "Hold it right there, honey." I'm trying to sound like Bruce Willis in *Die Hard*—*yippie-kay-yay, motherfucker*—but instead I sound like Kevin Costner in that Indian movie, too-serious and doomed.

"What do you want?" Tawny says.

"I have something for you," I say. "Something you need to remember about." I keep the lighter pointed at Brad.

"Is that your lighter?" she says.

I pretend I'm going to shoot and she pauses, looks at my eyes real close. She nods and says quiet to Brad, "Don't worry, he wouldn't hurt me."

Brad makes his Clint Face again, but he doesn't say a thing.

I lead her out the side exit and back a little path heading away from the lake. It's hard to walk, everything all jumbled and my legs working funny. The jean jacket feels like a suit of armor. I just need to sit her down, play the songs, make her realize it was always me and her, all along.

She walks slow and I have to jab her along with the pistol lighter. We move uphill until we get to a little clearing. I motion for her to sit, then plop down next to her. My vision is funny, everything slanting away and moving. "Tawny," I say, "we were meant to be together. I just want you to hear this, hear these songs, and you'll know…" I push play and Night Ranger echoes tinny through the woods.

"That's a nice song," she says. "But this isn't gonna work, Wayne. You're in trouble, you should let me go before it gets worse."

"It's our song."

She doesn't say anything. I reach for her hand and she pulls it away. "This is, like, kidnapping or something, Wayne," she says.

I can't think of anything to say to that so I turn up the volume. Night Ranger comes into the chorus, "…*motorin', what's your price for flight.*" I try to stand up but it's too much. I sink back and lean my head against a pine.

"I'm gonna get up now," she says. She backs away slow, her arms feeling behind for trees, her eyes locked on me. I wave the lighter once but she keeps moving back steady, getting smaller, a white blurry ghost against the black trees, until I can't see her at all.

I push myself against the tree. I take a few steps and stumble, then get up again and keep moving. When I turn around, I can see the lodge glowing pink in the distance. I sit down again. My breath sounds funny in my head, like it's coming from out of the woods, mixing with the cricket buzz and the sirens in the distance. Something crunches in front of me and I can't tell whether it's a squirrel or a bear or a man. I lean my head back. Another crunch and I look up, hold the lighter toward the noise.

A deer steps into the clearing and sniffs. I hold my breath. It's a fawn, beautiful and young. She's looking right at me, her head cocked, sniffing a question that I don't have any answer for. It's a miracle she can even stand on legs so long and fragile. Her head is so small. She takes a step and I hold out my hand. She walks up steady and nuzzles my palm. Her nose is hot and moist.

She walks past me. "Wait," I say. She freezes. I fumble and hit play. Night Ranger crackles through the speakers. The deer takes off with a shot. I can hear voices in the distance, getting closer. I turn the volume up as high as it will go, lean against the tree, and wait for the music to take me away.

The Celebrity Orders
Room Service

The celebrity answers the door herself. "Fucking publicist is making a Starbucks run," she says. She strides into the darkness of the suite. There is an insouciance to her walk, the careless authority of an alpha hyena leading her clan across the savanna. The interviewer pauses. This room costs more per night than six months of payments on the Honda. He sucks a breath and follows the celebrity's skinny ass down the hallway, past piles of clothes, unopened packages, empty bottles, and full ashtrays. The celebrity does not make small talk. Finally she sinks into a couch. She opens a bottle of water, reads a message on her phone. "So?" she says.

The interviewer has been given very strict guidelines—he is to focus on the album, he is not to discuss the sex tape, the issue of panties and proper technique for exiting an automobile, the failed TV pilot, the "thing with Britney," or "what happened Monday night." The interviewer doesn't even know what happened Monday night. He is from a small arts magazine, not necessarily obscure, but still, not the kind of gig that regularly sees him stepping into the mauve cocoon of the Chateau Marmont.

"So?" the celebrity says again. "Are you going to fucking start asking questions or what?" She is tiny, wiry even, with a bad energy about her, like a short sailor a few hours into a bender.

The interviewer fumbles with his recorder, he looks at his notes. "So the new album…" he starts.

"Are you hungry?" the celebrity says. "I'm fucking starving. Let's order room service."

• • •

The celebrity is different from us. Her heart beats faster. Her blood, thinner. Arms, legs, torso, ankles, fingers, all more delicate than most children. Although she weighs less than one hundred pounds, the celebrity's head is significantly larger than yours or mine.

• • •

Room service arrives. The celebrity has ordered smoked salmon, two pancakes, roast chicken with black truffles, fresh kiwi, three orders of ahi tuna, onion rings, a bottle of Clos du Mesnil, three cans of Red Bull, four t-bones, and a grilled fennel and mushroom omelette. "Do you have any money?" she asks the interviewer. The bellman stands erect by the door.

"Um…." the interviewer stammers. He has forty dollars in his wallet. He gets paid six days from now. He has two hundred and ten dollars to last six days. This should not be a problem. He is comfortable. The work at the magazine pays well for what it is, even if he is forced to rent in a less fashionable part of the city.

The celebrity smiles. The interviewer remembers what a bad actress the celebrity is. He has seen the TV pilot. He knows a little about the celebrity, the sharp bark of her laugh, what she is likely to say later on, in the limo, on her way to one place or another. He looks at the room service cart. Surely this is more than two hundred and ten dollars, more than five hundred, maybe a thousand. How much does a bottle of Clos du Mesnil cost, room service? "Not really," he says, patting his wallet. "Not on me."

"No money at all?" The celebrity speaks like a supervisor who has caught him in a lie. There is a punchline in her voice, as if she's gained some kind of advantage, like a courtroom lawyer about to shout "Aha!"

The interviewer feels the heat rise to his cheeks. "No money at all," he says. "Do you?"

"Do I?" the celebrity says. Her eyes register disbelief. She smiles, snorts a laugh. "Fucking. What? *Do I?*" She shifts in her chair, jumping closer. The interviewer knows all about body language, but he cannot help himself. He pulls back. "Do I have any money?" she says. "You really don't know what the fuck's going on at all, do you?"

• • •

The celebrity has spent very little of her young life waiting. She is rarely stuck in traffic, is almost never required to linger in any kind of queue. She has never seen the inside of a Department of Motor Vehicles, hasn't been in a grocery store for a decade. If she could change anything about Los Angeles, it would be to quadruple the size of the women's bathroom in the Viper Room.

• • •

The celebrity makes several calls from her mobile phone while the interviewer waits. The publicist is stranded on Sunset. Other people are not answering their phones. Nobody has money, not *actual* money. "Fuck, okay," the celebrity says. She nods her head, as if she is trying to convince herself. "I'll just call the number then, it'll be cool."

"The number?" the interviewer says.

She pauses, makes a face. She is young. The interviewer knew this coming in. But she is also tiny. She is a child. "Um…yeah… *the number*," she says, as if she is describing the most obvious thing in the world. She fishes in her Balenciaga bag, places twenty scraps of paper on the bed. She sorts through them, offering comments on each item: "…That kid is a fucker…stupid bitch…firecrotch…he is sooooo talented…" Finally, she seizes on a card, a single phone number printed in large type. She punches the digits into the phone. "It's me," she says, her voice ratcheting smoothly into a register the interviewer might call sweet. "I need more money."

• • •

In the back of the celebrity's mind, every now and then, doubt flickers like a dying firefly. Why am I famous? What do I actually *do*? How long can this possibly last? This happens very infrequently, almost always after she has come into direct contact with Bono or Angelina Jolie.

• • •

"I need to what?" the celebrity shouts into the phone. "With who?" She sits up. For the first time, she looks legitimately

144

concerned. This countenance does not fit well. It is, the interviewer thinks, like one of those little girls in a beauty contest, shaking her ass in some kind of imitation of an imitation of something. She covers the phone with a tiny hand. "Who is Manu Ginobli?" she says.

The interviewer smiles. What game is the celebrity playing? "He plays for the San Antonio Spurs."

"The San Antonio fucking Spurs!" the celebrity yells at the phone. "Like I'm gonna date a fucking San Antonio Spur!"

"He's pretty good," the interviewer says.

"At least somebody from the Lakers," the celebrity says. The other party is still talking. "Ten pounds?" she says. "Ten? Fuck, how am I gonna gain ten pounds?" The interviewer can hear the other end of the line—a deep, calm, male voice, like an old time movie star. "Fifteen? Fuck! No, okay—no talking back. Fifteen pounds? Do you know what I'm gonna have to do to gain *fifteen pounds*?"

• • •

The celebrity has always been a celebrity. She is the child of a singer and an actor. She is, one could say, to the tabloids born. When she sees herself in *US Weekly* or *In Touch*, on *Hollywood Extra* or *Access Hollywood*, Gawker or Defamer or PerezHilton.com, it is as natural as looking at the back of her own hand.

When she looks at these magazines and tabloids, the gossip websites and late night comedy shows, and does not see herself, her smartass grin, grinning right back at her, the effect is jarring, like looking into a perfectly blank mirror.

145

• • •

"Is that how it always works?" the interviewer says. He wishes, just for a brief moment, that he had some kind of accent. Australian would be nice. "With the money?"

"What?" the celebrity says. "No. Sometimes. I mean, the number is always different."

"Who gives you the number?"

"This is a hard one, though. I mean, fuck, how am I going to gain fifteen pounds?"

"So when you call…" The interviewer trails off. I'm on to something, he thinks. This might be the key: write a few thousand words, maybe sell something to *Esquire*, finally, or the *New Yorker*.

"Like I'm gonna give you the number."

"That's not what I mean," he says. "More like, how does it work? When did you first get the number, where does the money come from?" At the very least, the magazine will appreciate this. Certainly, there will be a promotion, other offers, more money. An editorial post, perhaps. An agent. A book deal. High six figures at auction. Movie rights. George Clooney will play the interviewer, or perhaps that new blond Bond. Maybe next time I walk into one of these hotel suites, he thinks, I'll be the biggest name in the room.

The celebrity is typing on her phone again, making a face. "How do you spell fucking Ginobli?" she says. "Fuck!"

"It must be hard, what they ask you to do," he says.

"What? That?" She is checking her phone again, clicking through messages or numbers or contacts, her fingers pecking away. "It is what it is. I mean, I wouldn't want, you know, the opposite."

The interviewer looks at the plasma televisions hung on every

146

wall, at the expensive creams and unopened shopping bags that line the hallway. I could get used to this, he thinks. He sinks back into the plush softness of the sofa, puts his feet up on the divan. "What?" he says.

"The opposite," the celebrity says. She giggles, shakes her head affectionately. The celebrity, the interviewer decides, is very pretty. Small and too skinny, yes, but the way her hair cascades over her shoulders is captivating. Something about her is undeniably attractive. "You know, like you."

The interviewer lets his feet slide off the divan. He pretends to be stretching his arms, wipes a dirt spot off the smooth leather. With great power comes great responsibility, he thinks. Who said that? Churchill. No, shit, it was Spiderman. Worse yet, Spiderman's Aunt. The interviewer has been living in this town too long. It is time to make a change.

"I'll make you a deal," he says.

• • •

The celebrity is a amazed and bored that people pay such close attention to her. On one hand, she cannot imagine following, scrutinizing, but more than anything else, *caring about* somebody she hasn't dated or kissed or hung out with, somebody she has never even met, a picture in a magazine or a talking head on a movie screen. The idea is funny and inconceivably tragic.

On the other hand, it all seems so natural. Of course people want to know what clutch she's carrying, who she's wearing or dating or kissing or fighting. This is as it has always been. *C'est la vie.* It is what it is.

147

• • •

The interviewer gets home as fast as he can. He drinks three quarters of a bottle of Yellowtail while he stares at the number, punching every digit but the last into his phone. He tries to decipher some kind of code in the numbers, writing down the possibilities on the back of the receipt from the Chateau Marmont: $1,368 for room service, and the celebrity hardly touched a thing, just shotgunned two Red Bulls and picked at her fries, then started in on the champagne. He Googles the number and nothing comes up.

Finally he finishes the wine and enters the entire number.

The phone stops ringing and hears a light buzz. He waits. Nothing. "Hello," he says.

"This number is restricted." The interviewer recognizes the voice from earlier: deep, male, older than middle age but not elderly, like the voiceover for a high-end car commercial.

"I just want an interview. I'm a reporter," he says. As the words come out of his mouth, he wonders whether they're true anymore. It's been a long time since he thought of himself as a journalist. The truth is that this is as close as he's been to real reporting, Woodword and Bernstein stuff, since he left his college newspaper over fifteen years ago.

"I'm afraid that is impossible," the voice says, sounding firm but bemused, as if he has asked to interview Santa Claus or The Green Lantern.

"Impossible how?" he says.

The voice sighs. "How did you get this number?"

"Um…" the interviewer says.

"Where are you located, sir?"

He remembers how the celebrity handled this. "I need some

148

money," he says.

"Right," the voice says, as if he is correcting a previous misunderstanding. "Right you are. We'll send a car along in a few minutes, sir."

"You'll...for the interview?" For the first time, the interviewer can see some light at the end of this. He wonders if he still has the contact information for the editor at *The Atlantic*. "Or the money?"

"Of course," the voice says.

• • •

The celebrity is surprised when they come for her. This has never happened before, actual physical contact, men in dark suits manhandling her down the hall and out the front door. When they make the walk from the hotel lobby to the car, they switch their grips, a slight adjustment, she notes, that makes it seem as if they are protecting her.

They all look vaguely familiar, like the cast from a short-lived cable sitcom about bouncers: one with a ponytail, a blond lifeguard-looking guy, a shaved head and goatee thug, and a Biggie Smalls lookalike.

The one with the ponytail and the nose-ring looks especially familiar. "Were you at Stavros' party last week?" she says.

Ponytail guy smiles. "No, but you might know me from *Pacific Blue.*"

"*Pacific Blue?*" She waves to the paparazzi, thankful that she's remembered to wear the new Heatherette shirt and the Seven jeans that somehow make her ass seem a little more full. The flashes flash and she waves as they sweep her into the car.

149

The bouncers get in on either side of her, the ponytail guy in the front. He opens the partition and sticks his head in. "*Pacific Blue*," he says. "The show about the cops on bikes? I was the gay one. I'm a little bigger now."

Fuck it, she thinks, as she sinks into the car seat. *What can they do to me, anyway?* "Whatever," she says.

She is feeling better, more confident, like herself again. Things will not be that bad. They never are. Plus, she's received three texts already saying that Manu Ginobli, despite the silly name and the off-brand team, is pretty cute.

• • •

The interviewer opens the door to four large men in black suits. "Come with us, sir," says the blond one.

The interviewer notices soup stains on the man's suit, a nametag-size spot on the left breast where the fabric is darker. "We do the interview in the car then?" he says.

The largest guy—a few inches over six feet, with a look like a Russian bouncer in a cold war buddy movie—pulls the interviewer out the front door toward a black stretch limo. The interviewer has no time to think. As they move across the cracked sidewalk, he hears sounds, faint and getting stronger. Crying. Wailing. It is coming from inside the limo.

The interviewer's head spins. Fingers dig into his forearm. His neighbors turn away, the old people scared and indifferent, the teenagers giggling. They lead him to the limo, open the door, and the celebrity bursts out of the darkness like a cougar. She scratches the interviewer's face, knees him in the balls. The men in suits form a loose circle around her. She feints at them and they jump.

150

She is all sinew and adrenalin, jerking from side to side, a skinny gremlin in designer jeans.

"What do you guys want?" the celebrity says. She pulls up her shirt to reveal a breast, small and ill-formed, which reminds the interviewer of nothing so much as a newborn baby bird. "You like that, huh?" she says. She smiles, coy now, coquettish. "That what you want, huh, a little of this action?" She puts a hand on the place where her jeans bunch around her behind.

The men take a few steps back. "Come on now," the one with the ponytail says. "We're big fans. This is all going to be okay if you just act businesslike and whatnot."

"Businesslike?" she scoffs. "What fucking business are you in? The asshole ponytail business? The business of being a former fucking gay bike cop?"

The ponytail guy rubs a hand across his head. "Jeez, that's mean," he says.

"Hey, this might not be the best time and all," the bald one with the goatee says, "but…" he reaches into his jacket. "It's not a full script of anything, you know, just a treatment."

"Oh yeah," she says. "Sure, I'd love to read it." He hands her the document and she feigns wiping her behind with it. "Fucking script? Fucking gay bike cop? What the fuck else you have for me?"

All of the sudden, she seems gigantic, a tornado of curse words and airbrushed tan. It is as if she has grown ten feet, like a hero in an adventure movie, Patrick Swayze demolishing a barroom full of miscreants. A crowd has formed and cheers her on. She waves, smiles, sweeps the hair out of her eyes. The interviewer notices how it gleams in the sun, like something ethereal and molten and very, very expensive.

She turns to the interviewer. "Oh, so now you want something, right? What do you want? More money. More magic numbers? You want to get a little piece of this?" she grabs her other breast. "You want a part on the show, sing a fucking duet on the album, you want Justin Timberlake's home number?" She jabs at him with her finger, steps in his direction. "What the fuck to you want?" she says.

"This is more than I signed up for," the blond guy says. He keeps his hands up, backs slowly to the street, and melts into traffic. The others drop back, push their backs against the limo and stare at the sidewalk.

"Pussies," the celebrity says. "Fucking suckers." She texts something into her Sidekick. "And I want my fucking money!" she shouts past the security men, toward the front of the car. She turns her back to them and walks toward the street, her rail-thin arm high above her head, one finger signaling for a taxi. She doesn't look back.

Fall Apart

McGuire had been waiting to feel something ever since it happened. Of course, they'd sent everybody home from work. No point fussing over commercial real estate settlements when planes were literally falling from the sky, towers toppling, people hurling themselves into the space above Manhattan. From the eighth floor of his K Street office, they could see black smoke rising from the Pentagon.

Bannion handed him a stack of papers on his way out. "What's this?" McGuire said.

"Billable hours."

He steered the Accord up Connecticut Avenue and into the Maryland suburbs. It was a perfect blue day and he took off his suit coat, loosened his tie while he waited for a red light. He saw people crying in their cars, hurrying along the streets. Every now and then the cell phone rang, Amy checking his progress. There were rumors about another plane headed for the White House, she said. So many people dead in New York.

At home, they sat in front of the television. That same replay, the towers descent, clouds of rubble expanding in slow motion, over and over. Every now and then Amy cried or swore revenge. "I'm serious," she said, "you can't do this to the U.S. We will not tolerate." McGuire nodded and rubbed her leg. Watching her watch the still smoking rubble, he searched himself for some reaction, the way TV gangsters examined themselves to find out if they'd been shot in a crossfire. But every time he found, like those gangsters, that he was clean, unharmed. The same as he'd ever been.

Amy's family resorted to some kind of feudal communication instinct, small bits of information delivered one at a time. Her sister called to say there was a fourth plane down in Pennsylvania. The mother called to report on the whereabouts of a neighbor who had once worked in the Trade Center. The sister called again, something about suicide bombers and the Mall of America.

"Everything is gonna change," Amy said. "Nothing's gonna be the same ever again."

McGuire nodded, ran his hand over the golden hair on her forearm. He watched the rubble slowly extend, a cloud of cinder and ash and god knew what else pushing forward like a tsunami. He thought of the drywall dust, the way it had gotten into everything when they'd taken out the old kitchen. They had only removed two walls, some old cabinets, but the stuff had covered them like soot for months. McGuire had almost gotten used to the feeling, like always being a little bit dirty. But Amy had declared war on the dust, protecting the new living room set, the dishes and glasses and all the other household things like a lioness defending her young. In the end, McGuire had to admit, she had won. He looked around. The house gleamed and the dust was gone. They might as well be sitting, he thought, inside a West Elm catalog.

Amy scooted up on the couch, watched the television. Onscreen, the towers fell for the hundredth time.

McGuire looked out the window. It was a beautiful September day, hot, but not too hot, the sky as blue as the background of those insistent TV replays. "I might clear out some of that bamboo," he said, nodding at a thicket that had sprung up between the house and the neighbor's.

"Bamboo?" Amy said. "How can you even think about that with all this going on?"

McGuire looked to the TV. There was already a logo: "9/11: A Nation Mourns" displayed in the left corner of the screen. "I don't know," he said. "The stuff grows like a foot a day."

"Sometimes I don't know what goes through your head," she said, and returned to the television while McGuire stood up.

"While you're over there," Amy said, "you can take care of that flag." She pointed through the bamboo to the neighbor's back yard, where a plastic American flag, sun-faded and torn, was taped onto the end of a barbeque fork that was, in turn, stuck into the side of a tree.

"Oh," he said.

"Real patriotic, huh?" Amy said.

• • •

First he took care of the flag. He recognized it—a real estate promotion from the Fourth of July. As Amy watched through the back window, he removed the fork from the tree, extricated the flag, and then folded it neatly. He didn't know what to do next, so he held it up to the window with what he hoped was an air of finality. Amy gave the thumbs up and went back to the television.

McGuire put the flag in his shirt pocket and surveyed the neighbor's yard. A rotting couch slumped on the porch. A tangle of vines had long ago overtaken any semblance of lawn. Broken bottles, boxes, fractured lawn ornaments, and what looked like

155

half-formed chickenwire sculptures were strewn around the thicket. Through the bamboo, he caught glimpses of his own yard, green and ordered, trimmed, whacked, and mowed into submission. Just fifteen yards to the left stood the patio furniture Amy had shopped for so religiously only a few years earlier.

The houses were almost identical—"contemporaries," they were called, boxes of glass and wood that had been designed by a Frank Lloyd Wright acolyte in the Fifties. There were about thirty such houses, all tucked at various angles into woody lots of a quarter or a third of an acre. The neighborhood was what his colleagues might call "transitional," and along the narrow streets the Jettas of young professionals sat side by side with older, working class trucks and motorcycles.

McGuire made his way to the neighbor's patio. A boombox sat amid a heap of warping CDs. He pressed play and jumped when AC/DC cranked through the system. A song he recognized from college. He listened for a moment. Had he ever really liked this stuff?

A guilty glance back at his house, but Amy was nowhere to be seen. He looked to the rest of the neighborhood. All was absolutely quiet.

I'm on a highway to hell, the music continued. The greasy guitar and the singer's rasp felt like an abomination against the quiet afternoon. He turned the music off and thought of the neighbor. She had been gone all summer and there was constant talk in the neighborhood about her whereabouts, the declining status of the house, county maintenance codes.

"I wonder where Natalie is," McGuire had said a few weeks into July.

"That kind?" Amy said. "Could be anywhere."

"What do you mean 'that kind'?" he had asked.

"I think you know what I mean," she said.

McGuire had often watched as Natalie came and went, jiggling in her little t-shirts as she carried groceries or a case of Budweiser up the stairs and into the house. They had been neighbors only in the most removed, over-the-fence definition of the word. The longest conversation they'd had was about her tomato plants, which she cultivated in the front yard. She was jabbing plant food into freshly dug holes, wearing a tank top and cut-off jeans, her hair pulled into a ponytail. A dozen tomato plants sat in their eggshell containers to the side. She was smoking a joint and seemed embarrassed when McGuire had come up the steps with his two lattes and the Post. She'd snuffed out the joint, stuffed it into her pocket, and redoubled her efforts with the plant food.

McGuire had recently turned forty. Not so young, he thought, but not so old either. He could hear Amy's yoga tape through the thin windows. "How's it going?" he said.

Natalie pulled the joint from her pocket and regarded it as a normal gardener might a dandelion or a slug. "I hate gardening, man," she said, and let loose a throaty smoker's laugh that sputtered out into a cough. She pointed to the tomatoes. "I'll run some over when they come out."

He nodded.

"If they come out," she said.

"Uh-huh," he said.

• • •

The back door was ajar. He pushed lightly with a hand, shouted "Hello." His voice sounded strange in his ears. Nobody answered and he took a step inside. The house was as trashed as the yard. Light blue carpet was smeared with dirt and covered in junk mail and moldy pizza crusts. Cigarette butts were stuck together in giant masses on any available surface and scattered over the floors and counters, pink lipstick smeared like petals at the end of their khaki stalks. Magazines were everywhere; newspapers stacked waist-high in a corner.

The neighborhood was absolutely quiet. No cars. Only birds and crickets and the occasional helicopter whupping across the sky.

In the kitchen a stack of magazines sat next to a coffee pot and a toilet paper roll cut with a hole and covered with foil, the half-burnt remains of a marijuana bud sitting green and black inside. The magazines were a mixed bag of women's fare—*Cosmopolitan*, *Jane*, and *Glamour*—and pornography. There had been a boyfriend here for a few months, he remembered. But porn? *Penthouse* and *Hustler*?

What else was there about Natalie that he didn't know?

He lifted a *Penthouse* from the stack and held it like a tomato he was considering in the market. He glanced out the window again, half-expecting Amy to be watching. He opened to a page in the middle and was shocked to see a picture of a woman urinating on a mirror. Another page and a picture of three women intertwined. These things had changed. How many years since he'd seen one? Fifteen, twenty. Since college.

His heart raced and he realized with a smile that he was nervous. He thought of his boyhood, sitting in a friend's garage leafing through issues of *Cosmopolitan* that were bound for the recycling center. That smell, mildew and paper and perfume ads.

In the distance, he heard a plane. Planes. They got louder,

closer, until it seemed like they were directly overhead. He ran outside but they were gone. What the hell was that? "Nothing's gonna be the same ever again," Amy had said.

I should go home, he thought, even as he was walking back into Natalie's living room.

He picked up the toilet paper roll and examined the bud inside. It had been a long time. Again, since college. He lit a match and held the roll up against his mouth, one hand over the opposite side. The bud smoldered and then glowed. His lungs filled with smoke. The taste was familiar – smoky, of course, but earthy and spicy, too. He held it in and then exhaled in a massive cough. It felt like his lungs were on fire, and then like they were being tickled from within. He coughed harder until the tickle sputtered.

A siren sounded in the distance and he wondered whether something new had happened. He thought about the towers, the slow, majestic tumble. Things fall apart, he thought. A name of a book. An album, a new one. See, he thought, I am not so old.

Another hit from the toilet paper bowl. He held in the smoke, coughed it out again. He stood and looked out the side window, through the tangle of bamboo, to his own house. Amy walked by the sliding glass door and he watched her move away, the slow bounce of her breasts, the yellow shifting line of her hair. It was as if he was seeing her for the first time after a long business trip. The siren whined in the distance. "We will not tolerate," she had said. Jesus, he thought, what the hell does that mean?

He walked back toward the sofa. Through a doorway that led into what would have been the guest room in his house, a pair of panties lay in a delicate white heap. He picked them up. It was a lace thong. Before he could stop himself, he was holding it up to

159

his nose. It smelled like mildew and carpet and....maybe a linger of woman behind all that?

Footsteps. He threw the panties down and made for the back door. Just as he reached for the handle, it opened. He jumped. It was a teenage girl, maybe sixteen, tall, skinny, and pale, with too much eyeliner and a silver stud in her nose. "What are you doing here?" she said. She seemed more confused than angry, as if she had simply gotten the wrong number on the phone. He stepped back and she walked into the living room. As she passed, he noticed that her eyes were red, her cheeks wet.

"Do I know you?" he said. He recognized her now, one of the kids who walked down the street before and after school. This one was always alone, singing along to her iPod or slumping down the road in a meandering line. More than once, he'd had to give her a polite tap of the horn as she trailed down the middle of the lane.

"You're the neighbor, right?" she said. "Nat told me about you."

"What are you doing here?" he said, trying on an air of responsibility. I'm old enough to be her father, he thought.

"I bring in the mail. While Nat's at the beach." She held up a pile of mail, then let it drop onto the floor. She produced a key. "I have one of these."

"Wait a minute," he said. "What did she say about me?"

She laughed, a sound that seemed more like a sigh, and mumbled something he couldn't hear. She walked to the couch and sat down, put her head between her knees. "This is just such a fucked up day," she said.

"I was just going to clear out some of that bamboo," he said. "That stuff grows like two feet a day."

She looked up. Her makeup had run and her face was covered

with black squiggles.

If you cleaned that stuff off her, McGuire thought, she'd be pretty. She reminded him of a girl he had loved in middle school, a cheerleader who didn't know he existed. It had all seemed so important then, catching her eye, watching where she sat in the lunchroom, who she chatted with in the halls. Like a radio operator in some isolated foreign post, he constantly monitored the landscape for signals that nobody was sending. There was a period, gray and solemn, when he had wandered the suburban streets, his heart heavy and overflowing with young tragedy. He had sat on steps, climbed trees, made poses of adolescent angst and heartbreak. What was her name? He couldn't remember.

"My brother's in the reserves," the girl said.

"He'll be okay," McGuire said.

"The hell do you know?" she said.

This is absurd, McGuire thought. What's happening here? Why am I not in my house? He stole a glance at the toilet paper bowl and then at the girl. He wanted to say something to make her feel better. "Things work out," he said. "You'll see. Even if it seems like things are falling apart."

She stared at him, said nothing.

"In the long run," he said, "it all evens out."

"The long run?" she said. "God."

He nodded. The girl started crying again. McGuire wondered if he should go to her, put his arm around her shoulder. He heard a car passing in the street, a brief snatch of talk radio. Inside the house, everything was still, quiet, the only sound the wet sniffling of the girl. She buried her head in the couch and cried, soft sobs that shook her body. She sat up and starting hiccupping. "Oh fuck," she said.

fall apart

McGuire walked to the couch and sat down. He leaned forward, put a hand on her shoulder. "It's okay," he said.

"It's not," she said. She hiccupped again. He leaned back and they were facing one another. Her eyeliner was still running and she looked, McGuire thought, like some kind of beautiful zombie, an extra from a television show about teenage vampires. She leaned over, put her head on his shoulder, and started crying again. She wrapped her arms tight around his back.

McGuire put his hand loosely on her shoulder, tapped up and down, the way he might pet an unfamiliar dog. He looked toward the window but could see only bamboo. Stuff grows so fast, he thought, soon you'd barely be able to see out the windows.

The girl stopped crying. Her grip tightened. "This is so fucked up," she said. Her fists balled and she tapped at his back, at first soft and then harder, until she was pounding, her legs kicking, her little fists punching between his shoulderblades. McGuire tightened his grip, wrapped her tight until the fit subsided. His heart was thumping and he heard a shaky gasp that he finally realized was his own breathing.

She stopped crying, opened her eyes. He didn't know what to do—kiss her, let her go, hold tight against another onslaught? She hiccupped again and McGuire released his grip.

She stood up, too fast, suddenly looking very much like a teenager again. McGuire watched her walk out the door.

He thought of Amy, alone in the immaculate house next door. He looked at the bamboo, the mess inside this house. A television was pushed into a corner and he noticed that it was still plugged in. He turned the knob and it crackled to life. Onscreen, of course, the towers fell. He heard the planes, getting closer. The roar filled his head and he turned back to the television. He relaxed, leaned back, and watched the smoke plume rise gracefully, growing, gaining mass until it was all he could see.

Notes for the Guy
Who Stole My Identity

First off, it is *not* a bad identity, no matter what some people might say. Not like every day is swimming pools and movie stars, but you could do worse.

• • •

Some places you shouldn't try cashing checks: the Giant, the Safeway, DJ's, the check cashing place out on Route 11, the In-Out-Mart when Pepper is working the counter.

• • •

The Baltimore Ravens Visa gives frequent flier miles and some kind of Marriott points, not to mention has this picture of that badass looking raven logo thing. You can't get any more miles or buy anything, really, until the max is paid down a little.

About these miles, just so you know? They don't even give them for real until you settle up—like, you pay a dollar, they give you a mile. So say you buy like a whole bunch of stuff so you can get enough miles for a ticket to Cancun to show Tammy you're willing to do new shit? They won't even give you the miles until you pay.

There was a Ravens floppy hat, too, came with the card and might be under the front seat of the truck or might not.

• • •

There's some gas in your truck. The red Dodge, parked out behind the apartment. The rearview is hanging off on account of Tammy's new boyfriend Riley broke it as some kind of warning. There's a cracked head gasket that's gonna need replaced soon.

• • •

All the bills and the mail are in a pile by the television. I think to the left there?

• • •

The biggest problem so far has been not a lot of good control over the money. And the computer which was supposed to make things better just made everything worse. I don't know how you did what you did but I'm pretty sure it had something to do with the computer and that goddam Paris Hilton video.

• • •

There's a bunch of points on your license. Six or seven? Maybe eight.

• • •

Zechman is okay. Don't loan him money, but you can trust him
on most anything
else.

• • •

Any dude who breaks your rearview then threatens to call the cops
and keeps saying "Respect the restraining order," with this kind of
about-to-cry hitch in his voice isn't, one, the one for Tammy, and
two, a real threat to kick your ass and, three, should know better
before he shoots his mouth off all over Kratzer County.

• • •

Places you worked and got fired and probably shouldn't apply
again: Wal-Mart, Dun-Right Landscaping, The Buttercrust
factory, Wendy's (Scott Robertson, prick, manager), Arby's
(Robertson again), the Amoco out on Route 11.

• • •

The restraining order says five hundred yards, but if you park your
car by the high school and then slip down that alley between Elm
and Market, you get through this little space in the hedges and
get back to where you can see Tammy's bedroom. If you walk
slow and there's no moon, you can get all the way up under the
window.

• • •

notes for the guy who stole my identity

You get these fits. Depression is what Tammy calls it. Feels like walking around under a big heavy sheet, everything dark and too-close and no matter what you do it just hangs on you like a stink.

Drinking helps a little. Punching something, breaking shit, helps a lot.

• • •

Try not to think about the black thong or the way she looked when she was on top or how her hair was all kinds of yellow at once.

• • •

Under the mattress, on the saggy side, there's a pistol. You can't feel it when you're sleeping.

A box of bullets is out in the glove compartment.

• • •

If you need a karaoke, do a Johnny Cash. They're all pretty slow, and even though you can't sing so good, you can do that low voice thing okay enough.

Tammy likes "Ring of Fire."

• • •

A guy with a name like Riley is not the kind of guy people are going to miss.

• • •

You do not know how to ride a horse. So far nobody has asked, but if for some reason somebody does don't just hop on up there and expect to be the Lone Ranger.

• • •

If anybody asks what you were doing the night of the 24th, tell them you stayed home and watched the *Magnum P.I.* marathon. If they ask what happened, say it was the one where Magnum got the team back together. If they ask were you alone, say yes. If they ask did you talk to anybody on the phone, say Zechman.

• • •

Start with a letter. A note. Be cool. Tell her you miss her but you're doing okay. Ask about Riley, if she knows where he went and how long, how she's doing, if she's feeling lonely. Ask about her work, her parents, the goddam yippy dog.

Tell her you quit cigarettes, stopped drinking, that you're looking for work.

Thing about a letter is, if you need to, you have a few days to try and make that shit happen.

• • •

Spread the word Riley's down at his parents' in Florida. Tell Zechman to tell Spigelmyer at DJ's and Reichenbach at the sub shop. Tell Tammy you heard from Pepper at the In-Out.

169

notes for the guy who stole my identity

. . .

There's a patch of loose ground out by the fishing hole near the railroad bridge. Turn right at the big stump and go back like fifty steps. Walk slow. Check behind you. Bring a fishing pole, just in case.

. . .

There's a few clean shirts in the closet, up on the shelf. She likes the yellow one. Wear jeans, but make sure they're clean. No boots.

. . .

Kiss her on the neck. Rub the tops of her thighs through her jeans. Call her Darlin' like you got just a little hint of a southern accent.

Tell her you can't live without her. Tell her it's fate, like Ross and Rachel, Buffy and Angel, or one of those Shakespeare things. Tell her he's not coming back. Tell her nobody could stand in the way, that you're the only one could ever love her like she deserves.

Tell her I said hi.

Voodoo Chile Blues:
Twelve Step Hendrix

1. Admit you are powerless — that your life has become unmanageable.

He doesn't like the smokes they've put in the studio. They're packed too tight, and deliver none of the cool buzz of the Marlboros. But he does like the name: American Spirit. He likes it so much he's decided that's the name of the album. *Jimi Hendrix, American Spirit.* If, unlike any of the other comeback projects he's started over the past thirty-five years, he can actually finish this one.

Of course, he wasn't sober for any of those records. Can that be true, he wonders? Thirty-five years since he's been sober? "There are drug users, tourists, dabblers," Burroughs once told him, "and then there are junkies. The secret is knowing what you are, then being it."

Or maybe that's from a movie. Since he's gotten into the program—really gotten into it this time—it seems like there are so many things he's not sure about anymore. So many things he didn't have to worry about before. All this taking responsibility, making amends, watching your back and getting your shit together—it is exhausting. It's like waking up and realizing he's stuck in a traffic jam, that he has been all along and the only thing that made him feel better, the only fucking solace he got from the waiting and the steady drip of progress, the little bumps that nip at him all day long like mosquitoes, was the fact that he was asleep.

He looks around the studio, at the knobs and the dials and the digital readouts, the empty computers that are buried somewhere in these machines, waiting to be rewritten with his genius—the thing they call his genius, that there are so many words for, all of them darting at him like flames now, at his fingers so slow, his mind that doesn't fly and sting anymore.

I am powerless, he admits, and he knows more than he would like to admit that it is true.

2. Believe that a Power greater than yourself can restore you to sanity.

He tunes his guitar, and then the others, the one P will use when he gets here, and the one for the rhythm player of the day, whoever that might be. He is told that most of them are famous in some way or another but they look like kids playing dress-up in their thousand dollar stained jeans, the washed out t-shirts that cost a week's worth of fixes.

He strums nervously, fidgeting with the thing, listening to the sound. He is stalling.

He looks around. The studio is neat and clean. Businesslike would be the word. P is the most businesslike producer Jimi's ever worked with. And that's basically the idea, he knows. Get the old head into the studio and treat it like a job, like this process of working through the steps, slow and steady and one day at a time.

He used to believe in the music. That was all there was, was the music. Then the drugs, but then it all got mixed up together, music and drugs, drugs and music, and where did one stop and the other start?

3. Make a decision to turn your will and your life over to the care of God *as you understand Him.*

He's heard of P's work in the studio, believes in a way, wants to believe, at least, that P is the man who can bring him back all the way. "It isn't an artist's world anymore" Quincy said, "it's the producer now. They got their own sound, you're working for the man and if you're smart—*if you are smart*—then you'll learn to like that."

"I don't know," Jimi said. "I'm not used to being nobody's gofer."

"You wanna sit back, do what the man says," Quincy said, "or you could try and be the man, make all those decisions, have the label people breathing down your neck. Money people. Public relations. Legal. Internet marketing, digital licensing people. You want all that, you can have it."

Jimi nodded. This was all about swallowing your pride, after all, each goddam step, another little piece of his pride, what he was still carrying around with him. "I'll try it," he said.

And P has been as promised. All business. Maybe too much. Maybe so much that it's barely about the music at all. Play a lick, then sit and wait, smoke one of those nasty-ass cigarettes while P has a little conference behind the boards. Two cell phones going at once, some kind of web camera streaming Jimi's fingers across some kind of private connection, pale kids with dark glasses taking pictures for the DVD packaging, disembodied voices weighing in from across the pond.

But he knows, is told and believes it, that P is the one who can deliver him, finally, to the next place. He believes because he has to, because this process has sucked most of the belief out of him and something has to fill in, like water oozing into a freshly dug hole. He believes because has tried everything, and there's just nothing else left to believe.

4. Make a searching and fearless moral inventory of yourself.

The last few decades have not been good. This he knows in his bones, literally in the pain in his side, his back, the way taking a shit has become an endless, humiliating ordeal, his cougar walk reduced to his father's arthritic shuffle.

He could count down his assets, the things he used to have, like that goddam partridge in a pair tree song: one bankruptcy, two wives, three terrible, half-hearted albums, four aborted tours, five overdoses, six trips to rehab, seven managers, eight houses, nine cars, ten children, he could go on and on, but all of it is gone now anyway.

Morally? Morally there wasn't much to talk about. He was stringing days together, trying to get from one town to the next, one fix, night into morning into afternoon.

This is the extent of the moral inventory of Jimi Hendrix, age 65: he is still alive.

5. Admit to God, to yourself and to another human being the exact nature of your wrongs.

"Look, man, we should talk," he says. P stops twiddling knobs, raises his eyebrows. After two weeks, P is getting less tolerant of delays.

"Can you shut off this stuff?" Jimi says, he points at the web camera, the phones P always has laid out in front of him like his own personal works. P clicks a few knobs, mumbles into the phones, and then holds his hands up in a question. "I'm not sure if I'm comfortable, you know, how we're doing here," Jimi says.

"We doing fine, man," P says. He clicks a manicured nail on his Rolex. "Only thing I'm worried about is *time*."

"It's just..." Jimi starts. He breathes in deeply.

Give me the serenity to accept the things I can't change.

His fingers play across the fretboard like prayer beads. He thinks about the session with Harrison, Buddhist monks tittering behind the boards like happy gargoyles. "You gotta understand, I..." *Courage to change the things I can.* "I don't know can I play this way anymore," he says. "Can I play like me anymore. The way people want to hear, way I used to. All that, you know, sonic experimentation shit, the wild man stuff. It's not in here no more." There, it is out. He hugs the guitar, pressing the side into his breast.

And the wisdom to know the difference.

"Ain't a problem," P says. He taps the machine, moves a knob up and then back. "We on it."

6. Be entirely ready to have God remove all these defects of character.

God? he thinks. Six stints in rehab, a month homeless in Berlin, a million tours and enough fixes to kill most of the veins in his extremities. Diabetes. Asthma. And now this. He's been through a lot, been through enough, including god. Defects of character? He holds up a shaking hand. Where was god thirty years ago when the character defects were hubris and taste for psychedelics and a tendency to never return phone calls?

7. Humbly ask Him to remove your shortcomings.

"Look, man," Jimi says. "That last take wasn't quite what I was thinking of, you know, the stuff in my head, it's...not that, not what I got down on tape."

"Yeah," says P. He sounds bored.

"I know where we are with that. And with the time. But the thing is...I was wondering could you maybe teach me how that machine works, maybe, you know, I can fix it in the mix."

"You bucking for a promotion?" P says.

"Promotion?"

"That's my job, J. My job."

"So you'll . . ."

P is listening to something in his headphones. He twiddles knobs, bobs his head, and Jimi can't tell whether he's listening to the track they've just laid down or nodding some kind of silent assent to the machine.

8. Make a list of all persons you have harmed and become willing to make amends to them all.

Noel. Mitch. Buddy. Billy. Mom. Dad. Clapton. Kramer. Chas. The Rolling Stones are still going, and for the most part the same cats, he thinks, and I couldn't even keep a band together for more than a few years. Noel took it hardest. The Experience was the best thing he was ever going to get, and he knew it, a spaceship he attached himself to, like a stuntman dangling off a helicopter.

He knows there are others. Fans. Groupies. Real musicians. All the record people and the promoters and the secretaries, the guys selling beer in the arenas, kids selling records. He ticks them off on his fingers until he's forgotten how many times he's run up to ten. Five, six, seven?

But then he realizes that after Chas the people are archetypes, kinds of people, not even specific men and women. Is that better, he thinks, or worse?

9. Make direct amends to such people wherever possible, except when to do so would injure them or others.

He looks for the scrap of paper, finds it balled up in a pile of receipts and notes. He dials the number and Noel's daughter answers.

"Look," he says, "that auction thing you were doing there?"

"Ebay," she says. "The online store."

"I'll autograph whatever you want."

10. Continue to take personal inventory and when you are wrong, promptly admit it.

"Nice take," P says. "That one was it."

"Can we do that one more time?" Jimi says. "I think I'm getting" close to what this should be like, what I hear, you know." He points to his head.

P says nothing, just moves his knobs back and forth. "I think we're good," he says. "Let's move on."

"Good?" Jimi lights an American Spirit, starts formulating an argument in his head. But he knows it's not worth messing with P. The man is in charge. Like Quincy said, if you're smart, you'll learn to like it.

"These cigarettes, man," he says. "Taste like shit."

"Organic," P says.

"Organic cigarettes?"

"Means there ain't no bad shit in there."

"Cigarettes are all bad shit, man. The whole point of a cigarette."

"Not any more."

Jimi sits back and lets the smoke settle into his lungs. Organic cigarettes. "So you'll fix up that last take?"

11. Seek through prayer and meditation to improve your conscious contact with God *as you understand Him*, praying only for knowledge of His will for you and the power to carry that out.

At night, he picks up the old acoustic and lights a Marlboro. He pours a glass of whiskey but doesn't drink it, just watches the way the liquid glows against the city lights that bounce in from the street. He picks the introduction to "Red House." It feels good, the old chords coming back, the easy feel of his fingers on the frets. He remembers the barnstorming days, late nights with King Curtis, laying back and letting the old man play. He runs through "Red House" and into "Catfish Blues." He bends the strings hard, pushing the notes out loud, jamming them into the air as fast as he can.

It is just old blues, workmanlike shit. Nothing Clapton or Keith Richards, Johnny Winter or B.B. King, John Lee Hooker, Elmore James, Muddy Waters—hell, take it all the way back to Leadbelly or Robert Johnson—couldn't have done.

But it feels good. Right. Maybe, Jimi thinks, this is who I am now—an old bluesman, nothing more, nothing less.

12. Having had a spiritual awakening as the result of these Steps, try to carry this message to others and to practice these principles in all your affairs.

Jimi finishes another take and leans back. He rubs his wrist. Getting sore.

"That'll do it," P says. He nods to a group of workers who have suddenly appeared and they start packing things away.

"Whatchu talking about, man?" Jimi says.

"Got what we need," P says. "Now we mix. Should have something for you to hear in a month or two. Should be out before Christmas."

"But we never even hit a whole song, never even got a full run on any of em."

"It's cool," P says. "You know how we do."

"I don't," Jimi says. He is getting pissed now, feeling the old adrenalin coming back. He can't tell if this feels good or bad. Mostly, it makes him scared now, feeling the strength come into his arms again.

He starts playing "Voodoo Chile Blues" on the electric. He is not thinking, not trying to pull some psychedelic spasm out of his subconscious, just playing, feeling the song over like a familiar tool. He moves the tempo along, his feet slapping rhythm on the floor. His eyes are closed and then he starts feeling the old feelings again, like moving in a car that's going too fast but he knows ahead of time which way to turn, and then like the car is picking up off the ground, doing loop-de-loops, now a roller coaster, and then like the coaster is coming off the tracks, and still he can hear "Voodoo Chile" kicking just below the surface like a heartbeat. It lasts he doesn't know how long, and when he finally comes out of it he is breathing heavy, colors pulsing pink and orange against his closed eyelids. He takes a breath and opens his eyes, feels the pain settle back into his hands and knees. When he looks up, P is nowhere to be seen. The equipment is gone. Jimi is the only one left in the room.

The Godfather of Grapple

"I need a storyline," McGuire says, "something that really pisses people off." The big man purses his lips and glares at the writers with the same promise of swift violence he delivers before flying off the top rope for his patented Boardroom Smash. "I'm talking fucking water cooler and I'm talking WrestleZilla and I'm talking now."

Gminski sits in his usual spot in the corner as the writers gulp and shift in their chairs. Ratings are down. More importantly, the stock is sinking and there is a feeling that, after the improbable up years of the Nineties, the American Wrestling Federation might be on the way back down. Gminski watches with the feeling of disgust and fascination he's known since the younger McGuire somehow built his father's barnstorming carnival show into a multimedia empire.

"What we need," says a skinny, long-haired writer who Gminski thinks of as Abbott to his fat partner's Costello, "is politics. Iraq. Afganistan. Nine-eleven. The whole deal." He sits up in his chair. Where did these kids come from? Gminski wonders. "Okay here it is," Abbott says. "We get a guy, tall and skinny, right? Put him in some kind of burka thing."

"Those are worn by women," Gminski says. Everybody stares. Gminski never speaks in these meetings.

"A man burka thing," the writer says. "Whatever. We call him

'Osama Yomama' or 'Saddam Insane.' We do a four-week arc, have it lead up to Philly, big payoff with the Homeland Securinator."

The room is quiet, waiting for McGuire's reaction. Gminski writes down the numbers again, the stock, the retirement fund, the mortgage and what they owe to the bank. No matter how many times, how many ways he figures it, they always come out the same: negative.

McGuire gives a thumbs down, sticks his chest out, and waits. This is the signal for new ideas. Gminski runs the numbers again.

"I did have this one thing," Costello speaks up. He's a chubby kid with rosy cheeks who looks barely old enough to cut lawns. "Something I don't think we ever did before."

"Hit me," says McGuire.

"The announcer," the kid says, "Gminski."

Gminski looks up from his doodling.

"What're you talking about?" McGuire says.

"We pull Gminski into the action. Everybody knows him. He's more famous than, like, almost any of the guys. He's been around…respectfully," he nods to Gminski. "He's been around forever."

"You gotta be kidding," Gminski says.

"Interesting," McGuire says. He turns to Gminski. "Dad ever think of doing anything like that?"

"No way," Gminski says. "Your Dad had…" He pauses. There is plenty the elder possessed that the son does not. Scruples. Loyalty. But there is no denying that McGuire Junior has a way with money. The 401K he instituted five years ago was the first of Gminski's life. McGuire Senior, god bless him, never would have imagined the AWF could be traded publicly, that the logo would be trademarked, copyrighted, worn on t-shirts and backpacks, golf shirts and jackets and thong underwear, a virtual license to print money.

"This is insane," Gminski says. "I'm sixty years old."

"Tell me more," says McGuire, pointing a thick finger at Abbot and Costello.

"We make him a heel," Abbot says.

"Are you saying he should actually wrestle?" McGuire says, and Gminski feels them looking at his five six frame, the belly, the bald patch.

"Like we did with you," the skinny writer says, "make him a management heel. Everybody hates their boss, right?"

"When we launched that story," McGuire says, "ratings tripled in the Midwest. Attendance went through the roof. WrestleZilla Twelve was sold out in two hours."

"So it turns out," Abbot says, "after all this time, your dad left half the company to Gminski. Everybody knows they were best friends, he's your godfather…"

"He's been stockpiling stock options," Costello chips in. "And now he wants it all."

"A violent takeover," says Abbot.

"You and him," Costello says, "fighting it out for the company." They high-five and McGuire smiles.

"Hmmmm…I don't like the idea of actually fighting him," McGuire says. They are talking about Gminski as if he is not in the room. "But there's something here. We tangle once, maybe twice, we do a technical knockout kind of thing—he pushes me off the stage."

"He electrocutes you with a microphone," Abbot says.

"That's good," McGuire says. "And then it all leads up to Philly."

183

"Lance, you can't do this," Gminski says.

"I can, actually," McGuire says, a dreamy note in his voice that indicates he's still working through the details, outlining the soap opera plot in his mind, tallying up spreadsheets and profit margins.

Gminski wants to speak but the idea is so ridiculous he has trouble focusing on exactly why it couldn't be possible. But here they are in the AWF's plush offices in New York City, lawyers and Harvard grads working through the same script ideas that were once generated over beer and peanuts in the dive bars of the midwest. Of course, anything is possible.

"I'll make you a deal," McGuire says. "Give me a four week story here. You walk away at the end. But you do it with a little extra bump. Call it a retirement gift."

Gminski thinks about Shira, the pain in his side that won't go away. He looks at the numbers on his sheet. "I'm not wearing tights," he says.

• • •

Reitz sits up in the La-Z-boy and cranks the volume. On the television, Lance McGuire is standing in the middle of the ring, shouting into the microphone. His hair is blown out like a figure skater and his pecs jiggle and poke at his skintight mock turtleneck. Reitz takes a slug of lukewarm beer and lights a cigarette. The hour is almost over. He must have fallen asleep. Motherfucker, he thinks, the only good thing about the whole week and I sleep right through it.

He finishes the beer and drops the can onto the floor. He hasn't put down the toilet seat, made a bed, or washed his clothes since Debbi left. How long now? He takes a dip of Skoal, opens another beer, tries to put her out of his mind. He reaches for the figures at his side, a miniature McGuire, the Hurricane, the Rock, Mankind, and the Homeland Securinator. He places them into the empty beer case. In his hand, McGuire swings off the imaginary ropes, bounces off the other side. He rises to the corner, readies himself for the Boardroom Smash.

Onscreen, the real Lance McGuire is standing on the edge of the ring, pointing and shouting at the announcers. The veins in his neck stand up like bamboo and his face is the color of blood. He reaches a hand into the first row and yanks the announcer, the old guy with the Jew name who's been around forever, into the ring. The old guy looks dazed, wobbles around in a circle. He's fat and bald with those little beady eyes and Reitz realizes he's hated the announcer for a long time. He turns up the volume. "Gminski," McGuire says, "you're living a lie. A snake in our midst!"

"Wait, Lance," the old guy whimpers. Reitz snorts. About time. His hand still holds the McGuire figure.

"When all along you've been plotting and planning! Behind my back! Taking over the AWF one stock option at a time!"

"Of course I have some stock. It's…it's a good investment," the old guy says.

"My father started this business! And now you think you're going to come in here and take over!" He pauses and the stadium erupts. "I got news for you Gminski! It's me and you! And we're gonna settle this now!" McGuire tears off his shirt. The crowd goes crazy.

Reitz sits up. The beer case falls off his lap. He clutches the McGuire doll. He can feel his blood pulsing, the adrenalin in his gut, a little prick of pain where the doll's nose presses into his palm.

The old guy backs up, smiling one of those 'let's-be-reasonable' smiles. McGuire runs past him and the old man cowers. McGuire bounces off the ropes and continues again past the announcer, who backs further toward the corner. McGuire bounds off the ropes again and all of the sudden he's airborne, a human missile, his arms pulled back like wings, his head a weapon of destruction.

"Yes!" Reitz shouts. He pumps a fist, squeezes the doll.

The old announcer falls to the mat and McGuire misses his target, sails out of the ring. He crashes into the announcer's booth and lies motionless. The crowd gasps, boos, cries for blood. Reitz holds his breath.

The little guy grabs the microphone. "That's right, ladies and gentlemen, I'm the boss now," he says. "There are going to be changes."

McGuire sits up. He holds a hand to his forehead and it comes away bloody. He tries to stand, passes out on the tarmac.

Reitz hears a crash and realizes that he is standing, has taken steps toward the television.

"And I'm telling each and every one of you," the old announcer points at the camera, "that there's a new sheriff in town. And his name is G-man Gminski, the Godfather of Grapple."

Reitz looks at the McGuire doll in his hand. A line of blood is smeared over the doll's face. He looks at the television. They are carrying McGuire out on a stretcher, his face covered in blood. Reitz opens his palm. More blood. Something is happening.

Finally, he thinks, something is happening.

• • •

Gminksi holds the script, looks around the empty arena, then to the ringside seats, where a massive man wearing tight shorts, a tank top, and a weightlifting belt awaits his delivery. The man's golden hair is permed and his face is tanned and lined, like a pair of old cowboy boots. "This is awkward," Gminski says.

"Dude," the Hurricane says, "you can't sell it for me, you ain't gonna be able to sell it when this place is full of screamin' bastards."

Gminski sighs. "I am the rightful owner of the AWF," he reads, "that's right, Lance, and I'm here to take what's mine once and for all…"

"Wait wait wait," the Hurricane says. "I need more… everything." He sits gingerly on a folding chair, which squeaks under his bulk. The empty arena is dark and cold. The Hurricane rubs his knee and grimaces. Since he retired from the ring, the Hurricane has hung around the organization in a number of capacities. One of the services he provides is "entertainment wrangler," an AWF term for acting coach. Gminski has known the Hurricane since the barnstorming days—the only reason he's consented to work with anybody on what McGuire calls his "presentation and believability issues."

"You just need to enunciate more, man. Make me believe it. If you ain't sellin', nobody gonna be buyin'."

Gminski looks to the blackened seats. "What am I doing here?" he says.

"Hey, dude," the Hurricane says, "you think any of us gets to choose?"

• • •

Reitz punches in late and hurries to the shed to pick up his stuff. The rest of the guys are already out, which means there's no way he'll be able to slide. What he'd like now more than anything is just to pick up the shears and the hedge-trimmers, get in the cart, and get out to the site before Baine has a chance to break his balls. He takes a dip of Skoal, waits for that first buzz.

"Look who decided to join us." The voice is high and taunting. Baine is standing outside the trailer, drinking from the Styrofoam cup that seems permanently attached to his hand.

Reitz puts his head down. He fingers the McGuire doll in his pocket. "Sorry about that, man. Thing is," he looks at the bandage on his palm, "something happened last night."

Baine holds up a hand. "I don't care you fucked Paris Hilton, Reitz, I don't wanna hear about it."

"Not like that," Reitz says. "Something different."

"One more time you're late?" Baine says. "You'll have plenty of time for whatever the hell kinda different-ass thing you want."

Reitz hears a voice. It's familiar and muffled, faraway but right in his ear: "Kiss my ass, brother, tell him kiss my ass."

"Kiss my ass?" Reitz says.

"The hell did you just say?" Baine says. He takes a step forward.

Reitz swallows the Skoal. What *did* I say, he thinks. What the hell was that?

"Something you wanna say to me?" Baine says again.

Reitz coughs. The tobacco churns in his stomach. He shakes his head.

"That's what I thought," Baine says.

Reitz bends over and throws up, a thin dribbly line of sticky tobacco. Baine laughs and slams the trailer door.

Probably wasn't really hearing anything, Reitz thinks, just too much wrestling last night, not enough sleep.

And still, he feels different. Something is moving him forward now, in a certain direction. He feels driven, the way Eddie Van Halen must have felt as a kid, locked up in his room with nothing but a guitar, the way Lance McGuire must have felt, surveying his father's smalltime operation and knowing that one day he was going to build an empire.

• • •

They have made him a cape. Gminski looks at it, long and black, made of spandex, the letters "GG" written in flowery cursive. He folds it into ever smaller squares, until all he can see are the tops of the letters. It feels slick in his hand, insubstantial and somehow illicit, like a gigantic crotchless panty. He thinks about Shira and the house. He lets the cape unfold, ties it around his neck, and walks slowly toward the arena. As he gets closer, he can hear the roar of the crowd, the calls of the new announcer.

He stops, leans against a wall, and takes another look at the script. "I'm gonna classy up the joint," he says. His voice sounds tinny and small in the hallway. He finishes the half pint of Beam, adjusts his cape, and walks slowly toward the noise.

• • •

Reitz takes another dip and opens a beer. He's pulled the chair up close. He can't miss anything. Not now.

Onscreen, the old announcer, the one they call the Godfather of Grapple, is walking around in some kind of a cape. Now

189

he really looks like a fag, Reitz thinks. He's shouting, or trying to shout. His voice keeps cracking and every now and then he stares at the ceiling and swallows, like he's thinking about what to say or trying not to cry. Lance McGuire is in the front row, the announcer's old seat, with a neck brace and one of those halo things attached to his head. He is sitting in a wheelchair and blows into a straw to propel himself around the side of the ring.

"Every wrestler will now grapple in a suit," The Godfather says. "And no swearing. No women in the ring. You've taken what me and your father built," looking right at McGuire now, "and you've turned it into a freak show of whores and steroid monsters."

McGuire blows into his tube, sending the wheelchair toward the ring. He bumps into the edge and bounces back. The crowd groans. The Godfather laughs, a sound thin and high like a cat's meow. The cape swirls around his back. McGuire blows into the straw and the wheelchair backs up, he blows again and it moves forward until he crashes into the ring's padding. "That's right, Lance! I'm in charge now!" the Godfather says. "And there's not a thing your classless crippled ass can do about it!"

McGuire fiddles with the laptop affixed to his wheelchair. He types for what seems like an eternity. Finally, a mechanical voice says, "I will be back."

• • •

McGuire pops his knuckles and rolls his neck. "So where we taking this?" he says. "Tell me how you get me out of playing Stephen fucking Hawking for two more weeks."

Abbott and Costello are grinning. Gminski swallows more Pepto Bismol. God knows what they've thought of now.

"All the way," Costello says. "We're taking it all the way."

"The hell does that mean?" McGuire says.

"All the way to the cemetery," Abbott says. "You are going to die."

Abbott and Costello high five.

"I'm not killing him," Gminski says.

"Interesting," McGuire says.

Gminski can't believe what he's hearing. It's out of control. The pain in his side throbs. "This has gotta end. I can't do this anymore," he says.

"Then, of course, you come back to life," Costello says.

"For WrestleZilla," Abbott adds.

"Duh," Costello says. They bump fists, like basketball players who have just completed an alley-oop.

"Hmmmm," McGuire says.

● ● ●

"McGuire comes off the top rope. The Godfather is down. Ooooh!" Reitz drops the McGuire figure onto the head of the Godfather doll. He wraps the little cape around the old announcer's neck. "He's…he's…strangling him…" The Godfather doll bucks and McGuire pops off him, rolls into the corner of the makeshift ring.

The door opens and Reitz jumps. The beer case pops off his lap and the figures scatter. He picks up the McGuire doll.

"Nice," Debbi says.

Reitz blinks, waits for the apparition to disappear. He has thought about this a million times, what he would do, what he would say, the bitter-funny put-downs and the snappy comebacks. But she gives him that look like she's disappointed but not in him, in herself, like how could she ever have said yes, then I do, and then played house those six months or so. Reitz realizes he doesn't have anything ready for that one.

She has lost weight and straightened out her hair. She's still wearing the Wendy's uniform but now her nametag says "Manager." Despite himself, despite the little acorn of hatred that sits in his gut like a rock, he can feel the blood rising in his penis. He fights a memory, the two of them, the back seat of the Plymouth, moonlight and Boone's Farm and soft, hot skin. He wills down the boner, pokes the McGuire doll against it like scratching an itch.

"What do you want?" he says.

"Still playing with your little dolls." She sits down at the kitchen table, moves a stack of unopened letters aside. She still has that way about her, he thinks, like a babysitter waiting for him to go to bed so her boyfriend can come over. "Jesus," she says. "Have you paid *any* bills since I left?"

"What you want?" He tries to put some menace in his voice but it comes out like a squeak. He imagines the two of them in the ring, taking her arm and swinging her against the ropes. He would bounce off the opposite corner, spring toward her. Would I embrace her, he wonders, twirl a little do-si-do, or would I swing a forearm across that pretty face?

She takes out an envelope, smooths papers on the table. "Divorce papers."

"What?" he says.

She sighs and he has the feeling all over again, like a little kid who can't stop getting himself in trouble. Definitely forearm, he thinks. Better yet, the Boardroom Smash. "Okay goddamit," he says.

"Envelope is pre-paid," she says, waving at the pile of bills on the table. "I know how you like to put things off."

Reitz watches the door go shut. Her busy little steps clack down the hallway, somehow sounding happy and pissed off all at once.

He finishes his beer, lets the can drop on the floor, and reassembles the ring on his lap. He balances the McGuire doll on the top rope, getting ready for the Smash.

"Something gotta give soon, brother." It's the Voice, the same one he heard at work.

"What?" Reitz says. He picks up the McGuire doll, looks at the plastic face.

"It's on you, man," the Voice says. Reitz looks at the doll and swears he can see the plastic lips moving, the muscles ripple and bounce.

It's true, he thinks. It's all been leading up to this. "Holy shit," he says. "Holy. Fucking. Shit."

• • •

"I said no tights," Gminski says.

"Just put it on," the costume woman says. "The big man approved all this already."

Gminski unfolds the tights. They are silky black, with tasteful gray pinstripes and white piping running down the side. He looks at the boots. "Spats?"

She hands him a top hat with "GG" stitched across the front.

"I'm not wearing a top hat," he says.

She drops the pile at his feet. "Take it up with Lance," she says.

Gminski feels a hand slap at his back. The Hurricane. "Some shit in there, dude," he says, indicating the next show's script. "The Philly show? Some fucked up shit."

Gminski points to the boxes full of hate mail. "You ever see anything like this?"

"Never quite like that." He claps a hand on Gminski's shoulder. "You're gonna be set for fuckin' life, man."

• • •

Reitz hands his ticket over and waits to be frisked. He's sweating. All around him, it seems, are families—kids screaming, parents making small talk. Young boys gathered in tight circles, shouting about the Godfather or the Homeland Securinator.

The security guard pats his hands over Reitz's midsection and waves him through.

• • •

"This is it," McGuire says. "Kill me tonight. Next week I come back. And you're riding into the sunset."

"Sunset?" Gminski says. "I'll be lucky to get out of here alive."

"Jesus, man, no need to be so dramatic."

"Dramatic?"

McGuire puts his hand out to shake and it swallows Gminski's. "You need anything next week, just call the place in the Bahamas," he says. "Now let's get this over with."

• • •

Reitz settles into his seat. He is not far from the stage. He watches the early matches with little interest. Finally, the main event. "Ladies and gentlemen," the chubby ring announcer screams, "put it together for the meanest, baddest boss in the history of the AWF, G-man Gminski, the Godfather of Grapple!"

The Godfather comes out in some kind of spandex pinstripe thing, with the cape and a top hat. The arena is drenched in boos. People are swearing and spitting. Reitz can't imagine anything louder.

"Hello, morons," The Godfather says. "Tonight, we'll be enjoying some jazz from Wynton Marsalis. Followed by the very classy Joyce Carol Oates, who is going to be lecturing your dumb asses about the themes of violence and isolation that recur in her work. Let's give it up for Joyce Carol Oates, people!" Reitz isn't sure who Joyce Carol Oates is but he boos and spits and throws his beer at the stage with the others.

All of the sudden the place goes quiet. People are pointing to far side of the stadium. Lance McGuire is crutching toward the ring.

"Some losers just won't give up," the Godfather says. "Will they, people?"

Lance makes his way to the lip of the ring. He drops the crutches. The crowd roars. He wobbles, finds his balance, and slides under the bottom rope. He slowly pulls himself up, like Rocky in a mock turtleneck, until finally he is standing on the edge of the ring. He extracts a microphone. "That's right, Godfather! You can't keep me down. I'm here to take back what's mine! I'm here to take it back for all these people! For my father, who built the AWF into what it is today! For everybody who loves wrestling entertainment! For the common man! The common woman! For the goddam United States of fucking America!"

He takes a step forward. And now the old man is running, bouncing off the ropes. He is small but quick, and he gathers momentum with each rebound. McGuire stands in the middle of the ring, trying to turn with his crippled legs, struggling to keep his eyes on the Godfather.

And then Reitz can see it coming, the final gathering of momentum. McGuire's back is turned. The Godfather bounds off the ropes one more time, gathers all his speed, and lands a heavy blow between McGuire's shoulders. The bigger man goes down hard. He hits the ground and bounces. Blood comes from his mouth, pools on the stage.

Reitz stands, reaches between his legs.

• • •

Gminski is dazed. Bottles and cups pour down from the stands. He can't distinguish the roar in his head from the crowd noise. All this time, and that was the first time he'd ever actually made contact in the ring. Funny thing, he thinks, is that it didn't feel bad. Felt kind of good.

He hears the sudden pop above the crowd noise. Almost immediately, everything goes white and he is on his back, feeling at his chest. Wet and sticky. Cups continue to rain down from the stands and Gminski relaxes, lets it go.

• • •

Lance is on his face, allowing the blood to soak and puddle. He is absolutely still, waiting for the guys playing the paramedics to get him the hell out of here. Bahamas, he thinks. It will be nice to have a week off, to be forced to lay low. He feels a thump on the canvas, opens an eye to see Gminski on the mat. "Fucking writers," he thinks, "are getting out of control."

Gminski makes some kind of sound McGuire has never heard before, a thin, high, rasp that bottoms out into a low moan. Somehow, he's putting this liquidy cough into his voice. McGuire makes a note to have the Hurricane work with some of the other guys.

What is taking the paramedics so long?

Finally he hears footsteps, the crackle of their radios. He opens an eye. They are tending to Gminski. "No, you assholes," he says, trying to not move his mouth. "I'm the one who's dead! That fucker is just off script."

They stop. He gives the look to the lead paramedic, a tall lanky kid named Jackson who has been to AWF training school six times in the past four years. Jackson stops pretending to bandage Gminski's fake cut, pretends instead to check McGuire's pulse. He pounds on McGuire's chest, wildly administers CPR. Finally, Jackson shakes his head at the rest of the paramedics. They put a blanket over McGuire and carry him slowly out of the arena.

A murmur goes through the crowd. McGuire can hear people crying, moaning, the whole place keening with a low animal hum.

Through the thin blue gauze, McGuire can see Gminski, laying absolutely still. The blood pool looks bigger. Interesting, McGuire thinks. The old guy has really come around.

• • •

Reitz runs until he hits the concourse. Behind him, people shout and cry. Inside the arena, the crowd has gone silent. He imagines the hand about to grasp his back, the forearm moving toward his neck, the bullet that will knock him off his feet. But it never comes. There's nothing but a buzz and a few arms grasping at the very beginning, and then running, and then nothing.

He winds up in the lower bowels of the arena. Reitz goes to the bathroom. He buys a soft pretzel. Everywhere, people are running and hugging and crying. Parents walk grim-faced toward the parking lots, crying children plodding by their sides. They gather in little groups, pointing and staring red-eyed at the television monitors suspended above the concourse. Reitz sees it and stops in his tracks: the paramedics pushing the gurney, the sheet-covered body, and in the lower screen, "Lance McGuire: 1956–2007."

• • •

There is almost no pain. Gminski does not waste energy writhing on the mat. He lies silent, still, watches the lights in the rafters growing steadily brighter. It's really not bad, he thinks, a twist ending to the dreary life story that seemed to play out forever, the last act dragging in a way that wouldn't get past even the worst hack writer.

Is this real, he wonders, or is this a script change, something cooked up by Abbott and Costello, reviewed by the lawyers, initialed by Lance in a last minute creative session? The lights are fading and the crowd noise slips away. He is not worried. More like curious. Is this a hit or a plot twist, he wonders, and how the hell would I know the difference, anyway?

Acknowledgements

There are many people to thank, enough to require some form of organization. Since my memory and organizational skills are both terrible, reverse chronological order seems like the safest way to go.

Thanks to Willy Blackmore and Jennifer Banash for believing in and publishing this book. I could not have asked for more supportive, smart, or cool publishers, and I am truly appreciative that (a) Impetus Press exists, and (b) they've chosen to publish my work. There aren't many places for those of us who fall outside the mainstream and also, somehow, outside the experimental. Impetus is that place. Thanks also to Susan McCarty, whose editorial suggestions improved many of these stories.

Many editors published original versions of these stories, which were inevitably improved in the process. Thanks to Richard Peabody of *Gargoyle* and Paycock Press, Aaron Burch of *Hobart*, Gerry Canavan from *Backwards City Review*, Ellen Parker of *FRiGG*, Joshua Mandelbaum and Suzanne Pettypiece from *Ballyhoo Stories*, Michael Martin from *Nerve*, Julie Wakeman-Linn of *Potomac Review*, and the staff of the *Sycamore Review*, *Gulf Stream*, and *Dicey Brown*. Jason Sanford of *StorySouth* created and runs the Million Writers Award, which brought some notice to the title story, and is also just a really cool thing.

The Barrelhouse editorial squadron—Aaron Pease, Joe Killiany,

Matt Kirkpatrick, and Mike Ingram—read and improved early versions of many of these stories, and made me feel less like a delusional crackpot with a laptop and more like a part of a community (albeit, a kind of weird one). Thanks especially to Joe, who was the first person to suggest that I look at these stories as a collection, rather than a series of lucky events or a trail of suckered editors. Steve Battista and Mark Charney read even earlier, worse versions of some stories, and helped me stick with writing at a time when, if it wasn't for their friendship and support (and a lot of dunkles from the Baltimore Brewing Company), I would certainly have thrown in the towel.

Although they have no idea that this is the case, John (Buzzboy) Gallagher and Gwydion Suilebhan inspired me with their creative spark and entrepreneurial spirit. Thanks, guys, for having the balls to keep creating art against great odds, and for showing me how to keep on keeping on.

I've been lucky to have worked with several talented and supportive teachers from the Johns Hopkins University Advanced Writing program. Thanks to Mark Farrington, Richard Peabody, Bill Loizeaux, David Everett, and Steve Kistulentz for the knowledge and support.

Thanks to my parents, Don and Grace Housley, and my sister, Debbie Cooper, brother-in-law Joe Cooper, and to Skip and Linda Wieder, and Mark and Lisa Liddington, for all your support and love.

Finally, thanks to Lori. I'd be lost without her love, support, friendship, humor, and the occasional kick in the ass. She is, quite simply, the coolest person I know.

About The Author

Dave Housley is a writer and web geek who lives outside of Washington, D.C. His work has appeared in or is forthcoming in *Backwards City Review, Ballyhoo Stories, Hobart, Nerve, Potomac Review, Yankee Pot Roast,* and some other places. He's one of the founders and fiction editors and all around do-stuff grunt workers at *Barrelhouse Magazine.* He has a M.S. in professional writing from Towson State University and is currently finishing an M.A. in creative writing from Johns Hopkins University. He has webmastered for the environment, human rights, the government, and for money. *Ryan Seacrest is Famous* is his first collection of stories.